Lori Schultz

To Keep the South Manitou Light

Great Lakes Books

A complete listing of the books in this series can be found online at http://wsupress.wayne.edu

Philip P. Mason, Editor
*Department of History,
Wayne State University*

Dr. Charles K. Hyde, Editor
*Department of History,
Wayne State University*

Sidney Bolkosky
University of Michigan-Dearborn

Sandra Sageser Clark
Michigan Bureau of History

John C. Dann
University of Michigan

De Witt Dykes
Oakland University

Joe Grimm
Detroit Free Press

David Halkola
Hancock, Michigan

Richard H. Harms
Calvin College

Laurie Harris
Pleasant Ridge, Michigan

Susan Higman
Detroit Institute of Arts

Norman McRae
Detroit, Michigan

William H. Mulligan, Jr.
Murray State University

Erik C. Nordberg
Michigan Technological University

Gordon L. Olson
Grand Rapids, Michigan

Michael D. Stafford
Milwaukee Public Museum

John Van Hecke
Wayne State University

Arthur M. Woodford
St. Clair Shores Public Library

TO KEEP THE SOUTH MANITOU LIGHT

Anna Egan Smucker

WAYNE STATE UNIVERSITY PRESS   DETROIT

© 2005 by Wayne State University Press,
Detroit, Michigan 48201. All rights are reserved.
No part of this book may be reproduced without formal permission.
Manufactured in the United States of America.
09 08 07 06 05   5 4 3 2 1

Library of Congress Cataloging-in-Publication Data

Smucker, Anna Egan.
  To keep the South Manitou light / Anna Egan Smucker.
    p. cm.
  Summary: After her grandfather's death in the fall of 1871, twelve-year-old Jessie bravely helps her mother take care of the lighthouse her family has kept for generations on South Manitou Island in Lake Michigan, hoping that they will be allowed to continue to live and work there.
  ISBN 0-8143-3235-8 (cloth : alk. paper) [1. Lighthouses—Fiction. 2. Mothers and daughters—Fiction. 3. Courage—Fiction. 4. South Manitou Island (Mich.)—Fiction. 5. Michigan—History—19th century—Fiction.] I. Title.
  PZ7.S66478To 2004
  [Fic]—dc22   2004017349

∞The paper used in this publication meets the minimum requirements of the American National Standard for Information Sciences—Permanence of Paper for Printed Library Materials, ANSI Z39.48-1984.

For Mary and Ben

South Manitou Lighthouse, Michigan

Louise Bass

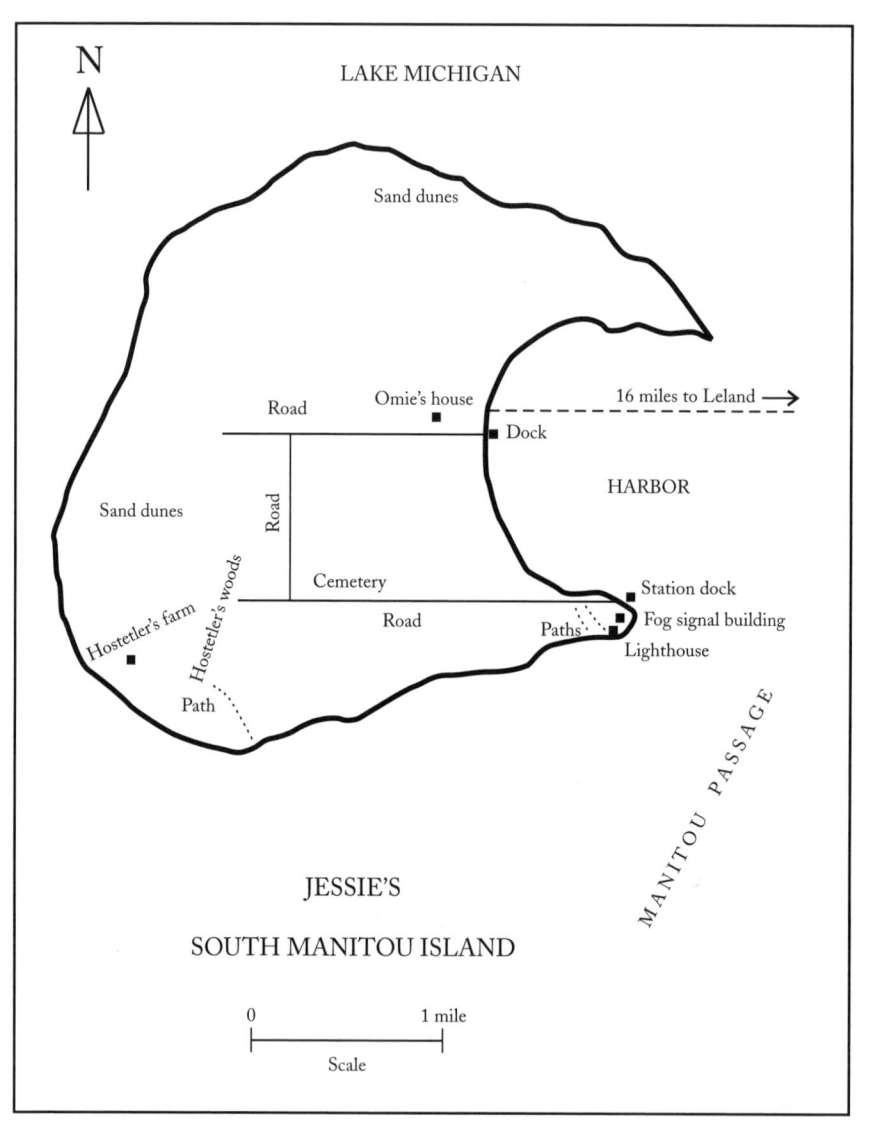

Jessie's South Manitou Island

1

Jessie grabbed a branch from the ground and hunched down behind the jagged, storm-splintered pine. She held her breath, watching, waiting. The grunting, scuffling sounds came closer. Never run from a bear, she reminded herself. What else? Hit it on the nose? With sweaty hands, she tried to hold the branch steady.

The sounds were nearer, louder, a snapping of twigs, crunching of leaves. Something was shuffling through the dark woods toward her. She took a deep breath and tightened her grip.

Then through the underbrush, Jessie saw the wild, gray hair with twigs and leaves stuck in it . . . the dusty, black clothes, layers of them, in tatters . . . the skin around a toothless mouth stained purple. Omie.

"I—I thought you were a bear," Jessie said, trying to make her voice steady. "You know, if I'd had a gun, Omie, I might have shot you." Jessie dropped the branch and shoved her trembling hands down into her apron pockets. She always dreaded encountering Omie. As she backed away, Jessie's heel caught in the hem of her long skirt and she found herself sitting in the dry leaves staring up at the old woman.

"Ach, ach," Omie muttered, reaching out a dirty hand, gnarled as a tree root, to help the girl up. In her mixture of German and English, *"Alle fallen down, alle fallen down,"* Omie said in a hoarse singsong.

Jessie took the old woman's hand, touching it as lightly as she could while still being well mannered. She wanted to say, she wanted to shout, "I don't play nursery games, Omie! I'm twelve years old!" Instead, she smoothed her apron and brushed the dirt and leaves from her skirt.

"*Ach,*" Omie said, "*fallen down,*" and opened her arms as if to give Jessie a hug. The stench of sweat, dirt, and foul breath almost made Jessie gag.

"I have to get back to the lighthouse, Omie," Jessie said, dodging the woman's arms and backing away. This time she was careful to look behind her, mindful to avoid any fallen branches or exposed roots, anything that might make her fall again. Then, turning from the old woman, she headed for the path to the beach. There were more twists and turns in it than the island's sandy road. The easier to leave Omie behind, she thought. When she was out of the old woman's sight, Jessie broke into a run.

When she was sure that Omie wasn't following her, she slowed to a walk. How many times had she promised herself that, just as she had outgrown her fear of the dark, she would outgrow her fear of Omie? But whenever Jessie came upon her, it always seemed that the old woman came too close, hovered over her. "As if I'm a chick and she's a mother hen," Jessie said out loud. The thought of Omie folding her in her arms made her shudder.

Omie was someone to be pitied, her mother always said. Even Jessie's big sister, Helen, who was terrified of garter snakes and mice, had never been afraid of Omie. For Jessie, it wasn't just the way Omie smelled, the way she came too close. It was the words the old woman muttered. Though they were just nursery-rhyme words, they made Jessie shiver as if the chill breath of winter were in them.

Stumbling at last onto the shore, she stopped to rest. Here the beach was littered with gray stones, polished smooth by the waves of the big lake. Even though she knew it was not a ladylike thing to do, she picked up a stone, round as a ball, and threw it as hard as she could out into the dark-blue water of Lake Michigan. Then, holding her long skirt up with one hand, she ran after a retreating wave to dip her free hand into the cold water. Scampering out before the next wave soaked her high-buttoned shoes, she patted the cold water over her flushed cheeks.

For a mid-morning in fall, it was hot, yet the sun that should have been shining brightly was dull orange, tinting the air with an unnatural light. Far down the beach, the South Manitou Island Lighthouse looked like a thick, white candle against the sky. A long, low passageway connected it to the lighthouse keeper's house, Jessie's home. To Jessie, the lighthouse was the most beautiful sight and the island was the most beautiful place in the world. She never tired of gazing out over the lake, watching the moving water. Now she looked across the channel to the mainland. Known as the Manitou Passage, the channel's dangerous shoals had claimed too many lives. Jessie knew countless more lives had been saved by the steady beam of the lighthouse, tended by her family for many years.

Across the channel she could see the great sand dune called the Sleeping Bear. She had always loved hearing her grandfather tell the Ojibwe Indian story, of how a mother black bear and her two cubs fled a forest fire on the western shore of Lake Michigan. Struggling to swim through the choppy waters of the lake, the mother kept calling to her children, but just before reaching shore, the exhausted cubs slipped below the water. On a steep bluff above the lake, the mother bear never stopped waiting for them, watching for them. When she died, sand drifted over her, covering her, and her sadness seeped into the earth, just as rain seeps into the ground. Manitou, the Great Spirit, took pity on her and raised up two islands in the place where the little cubs had perished. Called the North and South Manitou Islands, now they lie forever within sight of their mother: the great Sleeping Bear.

Jessie felt that in so many ways her island home, South Manitou, was a living, breathing being. Yes, it was the most special place in the whole world.

She sat down on a log and ran her fingers over the wood, weathered silver and smooth by the sun, the wind, and the waves. Though it was October, the wood was warm. It had been hot and dry all summer, and everything on the island was parched and dusty. Jessie couldn't remember the last time it had rained. Above the lake, a thin, gray finger of smoke stretched across the sky, a sign that more forests on the mainland were burning. There had been fires up and down the shores of Lake Michigan all summer, and often the heavy morning fog carried the smell of burning trees all the way across the Manitou Passage, all the way out to South Manitou Island. Years later, Jessie Lafferty would look back on this fall, the fall of 1871, as a time of fire . . . and ice.

2

Jessie had been on an errand for her mother, taking some salt and flour to elderly Mr. and Mrs. Hostetler. Their farm was on the other side of the island, two and a half miles from the lighthouse. There were no other people in between, except of course for Omie. The old woman lived in a ramshackle hut in the woods near the dock at the center of the island's crescent-shaped harbor.

As Jessie drew closer to the lighthouse, she scanned the dune grass for Henrietta, her best laying hen. Henrietta had been missing for two days. *If Omie finds her, she'll probably wring her neck and eat her raw,* she thought, realizing immediately how *uncharitable* that was. She knew that's what her mother would call it, but try as she might, she couldn't picture Omie doing anything in a properly civilized way.

Near the rocky base of the lighthouse, Jessie craned her neck to look up at the top of the white tower. Her mother was keeping the light now that Granddad was dead. Jessie still had trouble believing she would never see him again. He had never been sick, but on that awful morning just ten days ago, he had pushed his chair back from the table, put his hand over his heart, and fallen to the floor, dead. There was nothing anyone could have done to help him, Jessie's mother said. Through her own tears, she reminded Jessie that her grandfather, Patrick James Malloy, had done what he loved best, had gone about his lightkeeper duties to the very end of his life. There were worse ways to die, her mother had said, hugging her daughter close. But during the past week and a half, waves of sadness had washed over Jessie and she had cried until there were no tears left.

The evening before his death, Granddad had read to her the last chapter of *Treasure Island.* How they had enjoyed that story and so many of the others neatly shelved in the oak bookcase he had built himself. Just as Jessie had inherited his love of reading, now she had inherited his books, their old leather covers so powdery. Just touching them brought Granddad close.

Jessie rubbed her eyes. She wouldn't start crying again, she told herself. Her mother had just stepped out onto the iron balcony that circled the top of the lighthouse. Whether they needed it or not, the tall panes of glass that surrounded the light had to be cleaned. Jessie remembered asking her grandfather why. He had saluted and said, "Federal regulations, ma'am." He had taken his worn copy of *Instructions to Light-Keepers* out of the bookcase and handed it to her.

"Eighty-seven pages of rules, and most of them important," he had said in his pretend-gruff voice. Putting the book back in its place, he had looked straight at her and said, "Those rules are all well and good, but they won't give you common sense and they won't make you brave." She knew that in his estimation she came up short on both, even though he loved her.

"I'll make you proud of me someday." She had always wanted to say those words but had never spoken them aloud. Now it was a promise that she meant to keep.

Jessie looked up at her mother at the top of the lighthouse. Her mother was brave. She was also beautiful. Her eyes were as blue as the lake on a sunny day, and her long, brown hair was always caught back neatly with her favorite tortoiseshell comb. Jessie's eyes were no definite color at all. Hazel, her mother called them. Jessie's copper-colored hair was so thick and curly it was almost impossible to comb. Every morning her mother braided it for her into two long braids, often reminding her that she was getting to the age when she would have to pin them up, something Jessie intended to put off for as long as she could.

In contrast to her mother, who was so graceful Jessie always thought she carried herself like a queen, Jessie tripped several times a day, mostly over her own feet. And Helen is just like Mama, Jessie thought, and frowned. Helen, her big sister, had just turned sixteen. With her fair skin and beautiful dark-brown hair, she was as lovely as a porcelain doll and always acted ladylike. Helen had always seemed grown-up. Now she was over on the mainland with their Lafferty grandparents in Leland, sixteen miles straight across the Manitou Passage.

Grandmother and Grandfather Lafferty visited the island the last week of August every year. Jessie couldn't help smiling when she remembered their last visit. Her grandmother had pressed her lips together and shaken her head when Jessie's mother hesitantly asked if both Helen and Jessie could stay with her this fall to go to school.

"I'm just too old to put up with Jessie's shenanigans," her grandmother had said, making her voice weaker and shakier than it really was. "Now Helen is welcome for as long as you'll let her stay," she had added quickly, her voice suddenly stronger.

Jessie was so happy to be able to stay on the island for the fall that she had tried to jump over the anchor that decorated their sandy yard. That was how she got the scar that, under her long stockings, looked like a skinny question mark running down her leg.

It wasn't that she disliked school. It was just that the books in Granddad's bookcase were a lot more interesting than the stories in the schoolroom's *McGuffey Readers* about good children doing good deeds and bad children being punished. On rainy days when her chores around the lighthouse were finished, Jessie liked nothing better than to curl up on the window seat in the sitting room and race with Hans Brinker across the ice in Holland. She had read *Swiss Family Robinson* so many times the book had fallen apart. Now it looked like a package tied with string.

So Helen, her trunk filled with hair ribbons, neck ribbons, bonnets, and silk stockings, had gone to Leland, and Jessie was still here on the island helping her mother keep the light. It had worked out for the best. Now that Granddad was gone her mother needed her, not just with the chores that never seemed to end but to soak up some of the sadness, to make the house less quiet.

Jessie looked up again to the top of the lighthouse where her mother was hooking the ladder over the railing of the upper balcony. Her mother's long black skirt and white blouse were the same colors as the lighthouse. They made her seem almost a part of it. She is part of it, thought Jessie. She could no more imagine her mother away from the lighthouse and the island than she could imagine a sunfish walking upright on its fins down the streets of a town. Jessie knew her mother was miserable in the winter in the crowded house on the mainland. Didn't she start packing weeks earlier than necessary for the return trip to the island in the spring?

"This is where I belong, too," Jessie said out loud to an audience of gulls walking stiff-legged on the beach. At least she thought she belonged here, right here, on South Manitou Island. But there were times she wasn't sure. Her grandfather and her mother were so brave, the way they kept the light, and so was her father, piloting his schooner from port to port up and down the Great Lakes. But Jessie wasn't brave at all, certainly not around Omie—and, even worse for a lightkeeper's daughter, it terrified her to be up high in the lighthouse.

By now her mother had climbed the ladder to the upper balcony. As she polished the tall panes of glass, her black skirt billowed against the low railing. Jessie's stomach turned into a knot. She couldn't look at her mother, up so high, without holding her breath, without waiting for something awful to happen. Her mother turned to look across the channel, where the water had turned gray and choppy. Suddenly she grabbed hold of the railing.

"Jessie? Jessie!" she shouted.

3

Jessie cupped her hands and yelled up, "I'm here, Mama!"

"The inspector's coming!" her mother called, making her way down the ladder to the lower balcony. "His boat and the supply boat are only a few miles out!" She leaned over the lower railing to look down at Jessie. "I've just a few things to finish in the lantern room. Put the house in order, Jessie. Hurry!"

For a few seconds, Jessie felt as if she had grown roots. Then she ran as fast as she could toward the house. On her way, she grabbed the wet mop off the tree limb where she had hung it the day before to dry.

"Oh, where does it go? Where does it go?" There was supposed to be a place for everything. That was in the rulebook, too. And the inspector checked *everything*. Jessie raced up the curved steps to her bedroom and shoved the mop between her bed and the wall. Quickly she smoothed down the covers. In her parents' bedroom, she hung up her mother's shawl, which had fallen off its peg, and arranged all the shoes so their toes pointed neatly out. Then she headed back downstairs to the kitchen.

She had washed the dishes, but the big cast-iron skillet sat dirty and greasy on the sink. At breakfast, she had burned the cornmeal mush and had left the pan to soak. There was no time to clean it now. Where could she hide it? She opened the cookstove door and shoved the skillet in, praying that, just this one time, the inspector would forget to check there.

Jessie remembered how he put on white gloves to check for dust. He opened cupboards to see if all the mugs were in place, their handles turned the same way. He carried a clipboard and checked off everything. The stove was probably the first thing he would scrutinize.

Jessie imagined the portly man in the navy-blue suit, gold buttons, stiff white-collared shirt, and polished black shoes as he entered the kitchen, his piercing eyes not missing anything. He would go straight to the big, black stove and open its heavy oven door. And when he saw the greasy, crusty skillet hidden in there, he would throw his clipboard to the floor in disgust.

"Oh, where can I hide it?" Jessie had tried her best to keep up with the cleaning and care of the lighthouse, but she knew there were many things not scrubbed and polished as they should be.

During the summer, before Helen left for the mainland, both girls had helped their mother with all the housekeeping chores. And less than two weeks ago, Granddad was alive, busy with his work of keeping the light—washing the windows, trimming the wicks, the endless polishing of the brass, the painting, the cleaning. The station had always passed inspection with the highest rating.

Granddad! Jessie's sudden panic made her catch her breath. The inspector didn't know about Granddad's heart attack and death. If he found out, would he send a new family to keep the light?

Jessie had been born here in this house; so had her mother. The ship captains and sailors who sailed the dangerous Manitou Passage knew they could count on the South Manitou Island Light to warn them of the dangerous shoals and to guide them into the only good harbor between Chicago and the island.

"We can't lose the light," Jessie said, raising a cloud of dust as she swept the kitchen floor. "The inspector can't find out there are just the two of us."

Jessie remembered her mother's words to her the night after Granddad died: "If we're brave and pray, Jessie, I think we can do the work till the shipping season ends." Her voice had sounded quavery, not at all how she usually sounded. It had shaken even more when she said, "The regulations say that the inspector has to be notified immediately if anything happens to the keeper." Then she had stopped, swallowed hard, and said, "I'm just afraid if I write a letter telling the inspector, he will send someone to take our place, someone new to keep the light."

"But you're the keeper of the light now, Mama," Jessie had said, grabbing hold of her mother's hands. "You're not sick, are you?" She had had a sudden vision of her mother lying as cold, white, and still as Granddad.

"No, no, I couldn't be healthier, Jessie. You don't have to worry about that." Then she had straightened her shoulders and said, "Papa or maybe cousin Martin or someone else will help us next year. But right now we can't ask your father to leave his ship. His crew needs him till this shipping season is over. We'll have to get through the next two months by ourselves."

Jessie stopped her sweeping and just stood in the middle of the kitchen. The inspector, Granddad dead, the frying pan hidden in the stove . . . she shook herself, trying to clear her head, trying to figure out what she needed to do.

"Oh!" she cried. She had forgotten to ring the bell to salute the inspector. She remembered Granddad had always given the bell three hard strikes whenever the inspector was near shore. That was in the rulebook, too. Jessie ran to the door to see if the tender had docked and almost ran into the barrel-chested, uniformed man who stood in the doorway.

4

"Oh, excuse me, I mean—good morning, Inspector," Jessie stammered as she backed into the kitchen.

"Where's your grandfather?" the inspector asked, his voice hurried and gruff. "I must talk with him right away. Where is he?" His sharp blue eyes scanned the kitchen. "Well, speak up, girl. Where is your grandfather?"

Jessie began, "He . . . he . . ." She could hear her mother's footsteps hurrying down the passageway that led from the lighthouse to the kitchen.

"Well, where is he?" the inspector asked again.

Jessie's mother stared at her from the doorway, her mouth frozen into a soundless *Oh*.

"He's over on the other side of the island." Jessie's words came out in a rush.

The inspector pounded his clipboard. "I need to talk to him, but I can't wait around. This is the second station in a row I've been to where the lightkeeper was off somewhere else."

"Well, you are several days early, sir," Jessie's mother said coming into the center of the room.

"And with good reason," he said, mopping his face with his starched handkerchief. "The whole city of Chicago is burning down. Across the lake, the town of Peshtigo went up in flames last night. More than a thousand people are probably dead. The whole forest over there is still ablaze. But this is what *you* need to know: the winds have been steady from the southwest, and smoke and fog are making the dickens of a pea soup all over this lake." He stopped, stuffing his handkerchief into his jacket pocket. "The infernal smoke is already as far north as Frankfort. You'll be covered by noon. Who knows how long the fires are going to burn, and who knows how many ships are going to go down because their fool captains won't pull into port and wait it out?" His face was red with anger and his thick mustache quivered.

"I just came to warn your father to get ready. Tell him to make sure the fog bell is in good shape and to be prepared to man it day and night—the fog bell and the light both. It's going to be bad, Mrs. Lafferty, a smoke blanket all the way from Chicago to the Straits of Mackinac. Lord have mercy on any ships caught in it." He shook his head and was silent for a moment.

"The supply ship should be unloaded by now," he continued. "I ordered extra oil for every station to see you through to the end of the season. You inform your father I'll see him next spring, Mrs. Lafferty. And tell him to get someone on the painting around here. This station has always been one of my best. You help him keep it that way."

Raising his eyebrows and looking straight at Jessie, he said, "And I'm wondering where the biggest iron skillet is, the one that should be hanging with the others over there on the wall. It couldn't be greasy and dirty, hiding in the stove, could it?"

The color rose in Jessie's face, and she looked down at the floor.

"You're just lucky that I don't have time today for a full inspection. Shaking his clipboard above his head, he said, "Mark my words, this will never happen again." Turning on his heel, he stormed out the door.

Jessie's mother hesitated and then started after him.

"Inspector! Inspector!" she called, but he didn't hear. He was already waving his arms to the men from the supply ship, urging them to hurry. Jessie remembered her grandfather saying that the inspector was a good actor, that he really had a soft heart. But under all those gold buttons, Jessie couldn't see it.

A tall, dark-haired man Jessie recognized from the last visit hurried into the kitchen with a heavy box of supplies: tea, coffee, salt, sugar, smoked meat. Behind him came another man with bags of flour and cornmeal. Both were sweaty and out of breath.

"Good luck to you," said the dark-haired man, tipping his cap to Jessie and her mother. "Inspector's, right. It's going to be bad. Two ships have gone down already off of Saugatuck."

A whistle blast from the inspector's boat signaled his impatience. The men raced out the door and down the path toward the lighthouse dock.

Jessie and her mother stood in the doorway of the lighthouse. Over the rushing of the waves, the wind made a dry, whispering sound in the leaves that still clung to the cottonwoods. The inspector's boat was already headed out onto the lake, north to the next station.

Jessie looked up at her mother just in time to see her blinking back tears. Jessie touched her arm. "Mama?"

Her mother closed her eyes and shook her head. "When the inspector asked you where Granddad was, Jessie, I wanted to answer, but I couldn't. I opened my mouth, but nothing came out."

"I tried not to lie. I didn't really, did I?" Jessie asked.

"No, Jessie, you didn't exactly lie," her mother said. "Granddad's body, and I do believe his spirit, at least a part of it, are still on this island. But up in heaven, I'm sure he said to the nearest angel, 'That's my Jessie. She's a quick thinker.' You know honey, he always said that about you."

Jessie smiled. She knew that her grandfather thought she

was smart. She could do figures in her head almost as fast as big sister Helen. But she couldn't forget that there were some things that didn't please him. He knew how afraid she was of being up high in the lighthouse, and he knew her fear of Omie.

"I couldn't tell the inspector the whole truth," Jessie said. "I don't want us to lose the light, Mama."

"That's why I didn't say anything at first." Her mother hesitated. "Then I was going to go after him and tell him. But I didn't. Now I think I should have. If even one person loses his life because I don't keep the light burning or the fog bell ringing . . ."

Jessie didn't wait for her mother to finish. "We can keep the light, Mama, just the two of us. We don't need any help."

Her mother glanced down at her, distracted, then looked at her more closely. And Jessie saw in her mother's eyes Granddad's measuring look. She felt her face redden, and she turned away.

The treacherous channel that lay between the island and the mainland was a swelling sea of gray waves. The sun, now directly overhead, was just a pale, white light shining through the haze. The mainland, usually looking like a band of blue on the horizon, had already disappeared.

5

Inside the squat fog signal building near the base of the lighthouse, Jessie's mother carefully examined the bell's gears and chain. She had not even taken the time to make her usual noontime pot of tea, and dinner had been a hurried affair of bread and slices of cold corned beef. Jessie noticed the lines that creased her mother's forehead. They had been there almost constantly since Granddad's death.

"I need you to keep the fog bell ringing, Jessie. You are too young to have this responsibility, but there is no one else to do it." She shook sand off the hem of her long skirt. "If only Helen were here . . ."

Jessie lifted her head, trying to make herself as tall as she could. "Don't you think I'm old enough to ring the bell by myself?"

"Jessie, all I meant was I'd feel better if I knew you and Helen were doing it together."

"Mama, you know Helen wouldn't want to help even if she were here." Jessie wiped the oil off the bottom of the long-spouted can. "Helen doesn't like to do anything that might dirty her hands."

"Jessie!" her mother said. "That was unkind. You would do well to act more like a lady yourself."

Jessie looked at her mother's calloused hands.

Like the lake before a storm, her mother's eyes darkened. "Hands like these, Jessie, don't mean I'm any less a lady. And something else you need to learn, my dear, is to think before you speak."

"I'm sorry, Mama," Jessie said. "I wish Helen were here, too. Our house . . . it feels so empty, doesn't it?"

Jessie's mother nodded, her mouth pressed into a thin line. Turning back to the bell, she said, "Now pay attention, Jessie. The bell can't stop ringing for even one minute. In the smoke and fog, the bell can be even more important than the light. I'll need to keep the light burning so when ships get close enough, they'll know where they are and where the harbor is. We need to keep the light burning and the bell ringing day and night until the smoke clears."

"You don't have to worry, Mama. I'll keep the bell going."

"You will, Jessie. I know you will. The bell itself is in good shape. It's fairly new and there aren't any cracks in it. What worries me a little is this chain on the clock mechanism," she said, running her hand along it. "Your grandfather always took care of the chains. I don't want to risk taking the chain off and not having time to figure out how to put a new one back on. It should hold. Just don't wind it too tightly."

"You don't think we'll be covered by the smoke for very long, do you, Mama?" Jessie asked.

"If it's as bad as the inspector thinks it will be, it could be several days," her mother said. "It all depends on the wind."

Jessie grabbed the smooth wooden handle and turned the crank, and the fog bell clanged a warning note. Together, Jessie and her mother wound the mechanism, her mother's strong, warm hand over Jessie's small one, circling, circling until it became harder and harder to wind.

"When it begins to get this hard to turn," her mother shouted over the clanging, "just stop, even though the bell won't ring quite as long. We don't want to risk breaking the chain." The steady *clang, clang* rang out over the island and across the lead-colored lake.

"We have to do everything we can to save our strength," her mother said as they walked up the path to the lighthouse. "Try to sleep after you've wound the bell. Set the clock to wake yourself up in two and a half hours. Use one arm, then the other, when you wind the bell to keep your muscles from getting too stiff and sore."

"But, Mama, when will you sleep?"

"When this is all over and we can see the mainland again. And, Jessie, don't worry if you hear pan lids crashing. I'm going to take some up to the watch room and stack them on my lap. If I start nodding off, they'll crash to the floor and wake me up."

Jessie looked up at her mother and said with the hint of a mischievous smile, "You're a *good* thinker, Mama."

Her mother smiled down at her and for a second she looked like the mother Jessie remembered from before Granddad died, before she started looking so tired and worried all the time.

6

Jessie helped her mother carry the pan lids up the winding steps of the lighthouse. The curved white wall felt rough and cool as Jessie's shoulder brushed hard against it for support and balance. The thick walls muffled the steady *clang, clang* of the fog bell.

In the watch room, Jessie held the lamp as her mother slowly poured the oil from what looked like a long-necked brass teapot. Together they climbed the winding stairs up through the second hatch. This was as high as Jessie would go. Here she still felt enclosed and safe. She couldn't bring herself to look at the closed door leading out onto the lower balcony that circled the top of the lighthouse.

She watched her mother climb up the ladder to where, on its iron pedestal, the great lantern stood. Opening its brass-hinged door, her mother set the lamp inside. Jessie could still hear her grandfather's voice explaining the light to the rare but welcome visitors to the lighthouse: "See these prisms? They bend the beam of light, concentrating it. This lens is a Third Order Fresnel. It has a range of eighteen miles, strong enough to shine all the way across the Manitou Passage." Granddad was proud of his light and the way he kept it.

Back down in the watch room, Jessie's mother entered the date, October 9, 1871, and the time, 12:45 p.m., in the daily log. In her beautiful slanting script she recorded, "Inspector arrives with supplies. Smoke from Chicago and Peshtigo closing in. Fog bell started at 12:30 p.m."

For a while, Jessie and her mother stood looking out the window at the thickening haze. Sometimes they could see a bit over the lake. But just when they thought the sky might begin to clear, scarves of gray wrapped themselves around the lighthouse again.

A three-masted schooner appeared out of the curtain of smoke and glided soundlessly around the point and into South Manitou Island's safe harbor. Jessie and her mother both caught their breath at the sight of it. The *Isabella,* with Jessie's father as the captain, was a schooner with three masts.

When Jessie read out loud the name, "*W. B. Allen,*" Jessie's mother sighed.

"Let's hope that is the first of many ships that our light and bell will guide to safety. Be thankful, Jessie, that your father is sailing on Lake Huron and not Lake Michigan. Now try to rest. Do anything you can to save your strength. The alarm will ring in two hours for you to wind the bell again."

With her strong hands, Jessie's mother squeezed her daughter's shoulders and kissed her on the forehead. Jessie felt safe in this small, round, thick-walled space with her mother's hands upon her.

As she descended the curving stairway, Jessie tried to hold that feeling inside her, saying in time to the clanging of the fog bell, "Be brave, Jessie, be brave." As she got closer and closer to the ground, she became more and more aware of how small she was, how skinny she was, and how cold and damp her hands had become.

She thought of Mr. and Mrs. Hostetler on their farm on the other side of the island and of Omie wandering around probably somewhere near the dock. Only five people on South Manitou Island. Jessie wished her father were home. She wished that

Granddad were alive and well, smoking his pipe as he rocked in his favorite chair in the sitting room. "Helen, I do wish you were here," she whispered.

The heavy wooden door creaked as Jessie opened it. After pulling it closed, she settled herself on the stone step. The waves made a soft *chh, chh, chh, chh* as they curled onto the beach just yards away. Jessie stared across the channel toward the mainland she could no longer see. Somewhere over there was Leland's gray-shingled schoolhouse.

At this very minute Helen is probably helping the youngest students with their penmanship, Jessie thought. She had to admit that Helen would be a good teacher, so patient and so grown up. "I just want you to like me more," Jessie said to the hidden mainland. "I just want you to be my friend, Helen." How could two girls raised by the same parents on the same small patch of land in this great big lake be so different? Jessie wondered. Helen would be happy to stay on the mainland forever.

Out in the channel, a steamer blew its long, low whistle. Jessie stood and stretched. She rubbed her back against the white plaster wall of the lighthouse. She loved to feel how it curved at the bottom of the tower. She often stretched her arms around it, hugging it, and wondered how many people's arms it would take to completely surround it. When Granddad was alive, when Papa and Helen were at home, everyone was always too busy to join hands to see.

The clanging of the fog bell sent vibrations through the wall and shivers into Jessie. The sun was just a faint dirty-colored patch of brightness in a blanket of gray clouds.

Jessie had often walked in the fog that came silently in the night and lasted until the morning sun burned it away. But this was different. It was the wrong time of day. And it was the wrong color, gray instead of ghostly white. The smell wasn't the smell of fish and cool lake water. It was the dry, acrid smell of smoke. Just breathing made the back of her throat feel itchy.

Jessie walked down to the fog-signal building. The sound of the bell was so loud she held her ears. Everything was in order, working the way it should. There was nothing for her to do. She felt so jittery she couldn't imagine sitting, let alone lying down, in her dark bedroom with its bricked-up window.

Through the shifting clouds of smoke, she made her way up the path toward the house. A dark shape suddenly appeared in front of her. Jessie was too frightened even to scream. The smoke cleared for a second, and she saw that the figure was Omie.

The old woman moved her hands in front of her as if she were trying to swim. She leaned her head forward to peer at Jessie. Her expression was one of complete confusion, and Jessie found herself feeling sorry for the old woman.

"Omie!" Jessie said loudly, trying to make her voice heard over the sound of the fog bell. "Chicago is burning down. The whole town of Peshtigo burned down. And across the lake, the forests are burning. We're getting the smoke from the fires."

Omie shook her head and continued down the path, moving her twisted hands in front of her as if to clear the way. As Jessie continued up the path to the house, she thought she heard Omie's voice from somewhere down on the shore, her quavery voice mixed in with the clanging of the bell.

7

In the lightkeeper's white-walled sitting room, Jessie settled into her grandfather's rocking chair. Its cushions still held the sweet smell of his pipe tobacco. Across the room, on a wall by itself, hung the woven reed cross, St. Brigid's cross, that had come with her family from Ireland years and years before Jessie was born.

"Dear God," Jessie prayed, "don't let the smoke last long. Please don't let any more ships 'sail through the cracks' in the lake." Jessie used the expression her grandfather always used for ships that never reached port. Although it meant the same thing, it didn't seem as cruel, as final.

In the big, empty house, the only sounds were the rhythmic creaking of the rocking chair, the ticking of the grandfather clock in the corner, and, from outside, the *clang, clang* of the fog bell. Jessie wondered if Helen could hear the bell from the mainland. Does Helen ever think about us here on the island? Jessie asked herself. Would she be proud of me if she knew I was the one who had to keep the fog bell ringing?

The rocking motion lulled Jessie into a light sleep. She dreamed she was out in the smoke-shrouded lake steering a three-masted schooner. Everything was gray and still. She steered the boat on, dreading and yet waiting for the grinding, cracking sound that meant the ship was aground on a sandbar or had run into another ship that had appeared too suddenly, too soundlessly, out of the blanket of smoke.

The jangling bell of the alarm clock startled Jessie out of her dream, and she raced to the kitchen to shut it off. The hands on the clock said 2:45. Jessie walked outside into the smoke or fog. She couldn't tell which. She could barely make out the form of the fog-signal building, although it was only thirty yards from where she stood. The fog bell rang out its welcome, its warning.

Inside the building, the sound of the bell was deafening. On her next trip to wind the bell, Jessie promised herself she would first stuff her ears with some cotton.

She grabbed hold of the wooden handle and began cranking it round and round. As it became harder to turn, Jessie used first one hand, then the other, then both. She could feel the muscles in her upper arms tighten. She stopped before it became too difficult, saving her strength, saving the chain. "What if it does break?" she asked herself. "But it can't break. It won't. It won't."

Through the shifting clouds of smoke, Jessie walked down to the beach. She looked up at the lighthouse, its strong light piercing through the swirling smoke. She would be brave, she promised herself, but glancing up at the black iron balcony that surrounded the top of the light, she couldn't picture herself ever having enough courage to walk out onto that thin piece of metal hanging over empty space.

Sometimes she imagined that here, just over the sound of the waves, she could hear the soft voice of her Uncle Jim. Although she was only five when he died, she remembered how he had always found time to talk to her, read to her, and explain how things worked. She didn't know why Omie sometimes said his name as well as her own. *"Ach, meine Jessie. Ach, Jim. Alle fallen down."*

Jessie often had nightmares and would wake up sweaty but

chilled, almost remembering what had frightened her, but not quite. That was how Omie's words made her feel. When Jessie tried to talk to anyone in her family about her dreams, she couldn't seem to find the right words. Her family would look at her, as though she had disturbed *their* sleep, and then would quickly go back to their chores. Jessie had learned not to talk about her nightmares, which only made them worse.

The hours turned into one day and then two days, an endless cycle of winding the bell, carrying hot tea, an apple, or a slice of canned meat on a piece of stale bread up to her mother, and then sleeping fitfully until the jangling of the alarm clock woke Jessie to repeat the cycle again. Night was thick cotton that pressed against her face, and day was just a lighter version of night.

Jessie sat up in bed. Something was wrong. Something had awakened her. It wasn't the alarm clock. What was it? Then she knew. It was the silence—thick, dead silence. What had happened to the bell? Jessie was on her feet, running. She grabbed the lantern from the kitchen table. Its light illuminated the face of the clock: 9:00. Morning or night? It didn't matter; only the bell mattered. Why wasn't it clanging out its warning? Had Jessie slept through the alarm? Had she not wound up the fog bell long enough? Jessie stumbled down the path. In the dark, the light from the lantern made only a small circle of yellow light before it was swallowed up in the swirling fog and smoke.

"It is night, not morning," Jessie said to herself. "Why isn't the bell ringing? How long has it been still?" And her ears strained to hear, dreaded to hear, the sound of ships breaking up on the shoals, the screams of drowning sailors.

But all was still. Even the sound of the waves breaking on the shore seemed muffled. She shoved open the door of the building and, trembling, lifted the lantern high. What she saw made her heart stop. The chain that should have stretched stiff and tight around the grooves of the iron wheels hung dangling in two pieces, powerless to turn the gears that rang the bell.

Jessie knew that she had no time to try to fix the chain. She shuddered to think how many lives had already been endangered by this deadly silence. The bell had to ring. It had to ring now. With both hands she grabbed the rod that connected the hammer to the gears. When she pushed it up, the bell clanged out its warning. Up, down, up, down, Jessie pushed the rod.

Minutes stretched into hours. The palms of her hands were blistered and bleeding. The sound of the bell was deafening.

Jessie ripped off her cotton petticoat. Keeping the rod moving with one hand, she held the cloth in her teeth. With her free hand, she tore the fabric into strips and wrapped them around her hands to try to cushion them from the metal rod. In the glow from the lantern, she could see the small circles of blood grow into larger circles reddening the cloth. She kept wrapping until her hands were stiff, white mittens. *Clang, clang,* up, down, up, down. The lantern went dark, leaving only the blackness and the steady clang of the bell. She was part of the bell, she was the bell, and her only thoughts were its clanging.

The hours passed; the night passed. Jessie wasn't asleep, but she wasn't awake either. She was in a gray place beyond sleep and waking. She knew only the up-down motion that kept the bell ringing. Once during the night she thought she saw Omie looking in through the window, her head swaying back and forth, Omie grinning her toothless smile, Omie rocking back and forth.

Jessie dreamed she was rocking a cradle. If she just kept rocking, the baby would stay asleep. She dreamed she was in a ship with its sails furled, moving, moving up and down on gentle waves, waves that were rocking her to sleep in a safe harbor. She was . . .

Jessie's eyes flew open and her head jerked upright as she felt someone tapping her shoulder. Stiffly, she glanced around to see her mother standing beside her. Uncomprehending, she continued to ring the bell. Her mother gently lifted her hands off the steel rod. Puzzled, Jessie looked again at her mother. Her hair was in disarray and there were dark circles under her eyes.

"Jessie," she heard her mother's voice as if from far away. "Jessie, it's over. The smoke has lifted. We can rest now."

Jessie stared at her mother. Daylight streamed in through the windows. She felt as if she were sliding into a dark tunnel, and then everything went black.

8

When Jessie awoke, she was in her own bed. Her whole body ached and her hands burned with pain. Her mother sat beside her, stroking her forehead with a soft, cool cloth. All was still. No fog bell clanged.

"Jessie," her mother said. "Jessie?"

"Ohh," Jessie said, slowly turning from her back to her side. "What happened?" She rubbed her eyes, wincing as needles of pain shot through her hands.

"You fainted, honey. Tom Fullen carried you up to the house. His ship made it into our harbor last night. You remember him. He's an old friend of your father's. He wanted to stay, but he and all the other captains are running way behind schedule." Her mother smoothed back Jessie's tousled hair. "Are you all right?"

"I think so," Jessie replied. "It's just my arm muscles and my hands." Then she sat up in bed, suddenly wide awake. "Mama, did any ships go down? I mean, when the bell stopped ringing?"

"The bell was only still for a few minutes," her mother said. "I heard it stop, so I went downstairs to see what happened. By the time I reached the doorway, it had started again. I had no idea, until I saw you this morning, that you were ringing it by hand." She touched Jessie's hands. "No ships were lost on this part of the lake. And that's thanks to you, my brave Jessie." Her mother hugged her daughter close.

Jessie winced as her mother's arms squeezed her sore shoulders, but she didn't care. Had she been brave? She didn't remember having time to think about whether to be scared or not. It wasn't the kind of courage she had dreamed about, standing up bold and fearless in the face of danger. But the look in her mother's eyes was enough to make Jessie sink back into her pillows with a contented sigh.

Her mother lifted a steaming mug off the nightstand and held it for her daughter to sip. By the time Jessie had finished the hot beef broth and drunk a cup of sweetened tea, she felt her strength returning.

"We did it, Mama," she said. "Just the two of us. We kept the light burning and the fog bell ringing." Jessie looked up into her mother's face, and for the first time saw the exhaustion etched there, the eyelids heavy with the need to sleep.

"How long was it?" Jessie asked in a voice more subdued.

"Three whole days and three whole nights."

In her mind, Jessie saw the hands of the clock, passing hour after hour without bringing daylight . . . those night-days, day-nights that seemed as if they would never end.

Jessie realized with a shock that her mother would have to tend the light again tonight, and the next night, and the next. Jessie swung her legs stiffly over the side of her bed.

"Mama, you have to rest. Did you eat?"

Her mother smiled. "I've eaten," she replied, "but I wanted to make sure you were all right before I went to sleep."

"I'll be fine, Mama," Jessie said.

For the rest of that day, Jessie and her mother slept so soundly, so deeply that the alarm jangled for at least a minute before it roused them. Down in the kitchen, Jessie's mother took one look at her daughter's swollen and blistered hands and said, "I'll make supper tonight, Jessie. I think you've earned a night off."

"No, Mama," Jessie said. "I can help."

"We're having stew," her mother replied, placing the washed carrots on the cutting board.

Jessie looked at the knife and then down at her hands. It hurt even to bend her fingers. Using both hands, keeping her fingers straight, she picked up a carrot. With her front teeth, she snapped off a piece and then laid it on the table.

Most of the carrots were in chunks by the time her mother turned around and saw what she was doing.

"Jessie, that's not exactly what I had in mind!"

"Well, when mother birds need to feed their babies, they do it to worms, only they chew them, and swallow them, and then—"

"I know, I know," her mother said, laughing. "I know what they do next. You don't have to finish."

"I'm only using my front teeth," Jessie said. "See?" And she bit off another chunk of carrot.

Jessie's mother just smiled and shook her head.

It wasn't long before the bubbling stewpot filled the kitchen with a savory steam. Jessie had two helpings before she began to feel full. Never in her life had she tasted such good stew. Then she realized it had been three days since she and her mother had sat down together to eat a meal.

Jessie sighed. If she were honest, she would have to admit that every muscle in her arms ached.

"It's to bed without a reading lamp tonight, Jessie," her mother said as she cleared the dishes from the table.

And, for once, Jessie didn't protest.

9

The next morning at breakfast, Jessie couldn't help noticing the dark circles under her mother's eyes. After keeping watch all night up in the light, her mother was always tired, but she was never this silent. While she drank her tea she usually talked, teasing Jessie about her cooking, reminding her about the chores that needed to be done or instructing her on this or that housekeeping job. Her mother never tired of reminding her there were things Jessie would need to know how to do, and do well, if she were ever to be a proper grown-up lady. No, it wasn't like her to be so lost in her own thoughts.

Finally her mother cleared her throat and said, "During the night I wrote two letters, Jessie." Tea spilled over the rim of the cup as she settled it in its saucer. "I wrote to your father. I asked him to come home early if there's any way he can." Taking a deep breath, she continued in a voice that she tried unsuccessfully to keep steady, "I wrote to the Lighthouse Service, too. I told them that Granddad died and there are just the two of us here, and that we need help."

"Mama!" Jessie cried. "They could send a whole new family here. We could lose the light! We kept the light burning and the fog bell going for three days and three whole nights, just the two of us. Papa will come home, and then the three of us can keep the light. Oh, Mama, don't send that letter. Please don't."

Her mother's voice was steady now. "Jessie, I have to, and that's that. The mail boat comes tomorrow, and both letters will go back with it."

"Mama, no!" Jessie pushed her chair back. The legs screeched on the wooden floorboards. "Mama, you said we could do it—if we were brave and prayed, we could do it."

"I was wrong, Jessie," her mother said. "We can't." Gently she took Jessie's hands and held them in her own. "Jessie, look at me," she said. "You know that November means storms—snow and ice."

Jessie pulled her hands out of her mother's grasp. Pain shot through her blistered palms. "Mama, haven't you said this is the warmest fall we've ever had? If you send that letter, we're going to lose the light!" Jessie burst into tears, her body shaking with sobs.

"Jessie, now stop!" her mother said. "Yesterday I told you that you were a brave girl, and I meant that. But part of being brave is being able to see clearly what you have to do, what is the right thing to do, and then doing it."

"Even if it means losing the light?" Jessie cried.

"Yes, even if it means that," her mother said, her eyes bright with tears.

"No!" Jessie yelled and ran out the door.

There was a large rock near the shore that was shaped almost like a chair. It was the place Jessie went to when she was upset and wanted to be alone. Now she curled herself into its stony arms. She knew there would be no use in arguing with her mother. If anything, that always made things worse. But that letter to the Lighthouse Service . . . her mother couldn't, she just couldn't, send that letter.

In her mind, Jessie could see the family who would be sent to replace them. The father would be strong and handsome in his navy-blue lightkeeper's uniform. The mother would be smiling and somewhat plump. They would have sons, many sons who would take over the house, take over the island. Jessie and her mother would pack up their belongings and leave. Standing on the deck of the boat, they would watch as the lighthouse got smaller and smaller. They would watch until they saw their home disappear, the only real home the Malloys had known since coming from Ireland so many years ago.

Just as other children had grown up on fairy tales, Jessie had grown up hearing tales of the brave Malloys. Her favorite was the story of how Granddad, who knew the sandbars and deep spots of the lake as well as he knew the steps that circled to the top of the lighthouse, had saved the crew and passengers of a ship during a terrible November storm.

She knew the story by heart: From the top of the lighthouse, Granddad saw the waves rocking the ship, hopelessly caught on a shoal a quarter-mile east of the island. Knowing she would soon be torn apart, he raced down the winding steps of the light and up the shore to the point closest to the wreck. Cries for help mingled with the sounds of the wind and breakers. He tore off his coat and waded into the icy water. With the dark waves surging around him, he walked out on the hidden shoals. Finally reaching the listing ship, he yelled for the sailors to drop him a rope. Knotting it around his waist, he urged the passengers to climb down the rope ladder to him. Then he tied each in turn into the rope. When all twenty crew and passengers were secured, he led them to safety. By the time they reached the shore, the ship had completely broken up. Jessie could look out at the lake and imagine it all as it had happened.

Several times her grandfather, as well as her Uncle Jim, had almost frozen to death while searching the shore for survivors of other ships that ran aground near the island. Captains and their crews never entered the Manitou Passage without remembering that the stretch of water between the Manitou Islands and Pyramid and Sleeping Bear Points could become their final resting place. In their own ways, they silently thanked the Malloys for faithfully tending the South Manitou Island Light.

Jessie reached down to pull on a clump of beach grass growing beside the rock. The sharp blades cut into her blistered hand like knives. What was she thinking? She knew beach grass had roots as strong as an iron net spread out under the sand.

"No one can make us leave the island. No one can make us give up the lighthouse, not if we do our job, not if we keep the light burning," Jessie whispered, as two drops of blood dripped off her palm onto the bleached gray stone.

Jessie thought of the letter her mother had written to the Lighthouse Service. Then she thought of a plan, a way to send a letter that might take a long time to reach its destination.

10

The mailboat was late. To Jessie, it seemed that she had been pacing back and forth on the dock all morning, waiting, waiting. A stiff wind was whipping the lake, and the spray from the waves darkened the dock's weathered boards.

It was hard for Jessie to imagine that the dock had once been a scene of constant activity, boats unloading goods for the island's residents and taking on wood cut from the island's forests. The wood fueled the steamers' engines as they traveled Lake Michigan north toward the Straits of Mackinac or south toward Chicago.

That boom period had lasted only as long as the island's wood supply. When that came to an end, the island had been abandoned by everyone except the Hostetlers, Jessie's family at the lighthouse, and Omie. The Hostetlers, elderly now, still farmed their sandy acres on the other side of the island.

Unlike the other landowners during the boom, the Hostetlers had refused to sell any of their wooded acreage that formed the eastern boundary of their property. Although second-growth trees had begun to spread over most of the island, their wood patch was the only place where the white cedars soared into the sky, dwarfing everything around them. With a mixture of pride and awe, Mr. Hostetler had often told Jessie that those trees were growing on South Manitou Island before Christopher Columbus discovered America. He showed her how to count the tree rings on a cross section sawed from one of the giants felled by a windstorm.

A deep blanket of pine needles covered the ground under the trees. On bright days, the sunlight slanting through the branches made it seem a magical place, but on gray, cloudy days Jessie thought it was the darkest, saddest place in the world. She tried to squirm out of running errands to the Hostetlers on days like that.

Omie lived in a shack in the scrubby woods beyond the dock. To provide for her needs, she dug ginseng. She knew the damp, shady places where the prized herb grew. Whenever a boat docked, which wasn't very often these days, Omie appeared, lugging an old burlap bag that contained at least a few of the herb's gnarled roots.

The mailboat captain was a good man, and he looked out for Omie, giving her, for her ginseng, a fair trade of food and chewing tobacco. The mailboat, which came every two weeks, was the island's link to the mainland. Usually Captain Dave had a riddle or joke for Jessie and sometimes even some peppermint candy.

Jessie shaded her eyes against the bright morning sun and waved as the mailboat finally came into sight. For what must have been the tenth time, she checked the buckles on the leather pouch at her feet.

When the boat pulled up alongside the dock, no one jumped ashore to tie it up. Captain Dave waved to Jessie and shouted, "No time to stop and visit today, Jess. I'm three days behind on my deliveries because of the smoke. Chicago and Peshtigo both burned to the ground, and there's hardly a tree left standing across the lake. Did you hear?"

"Yes, from the inspector," Jessie replied.

One of the crew threw the leather mailpouch onto the dock, and Jessie easily heaved her lightweight pouch over to him. The captain tooted his whistle, and the boat pulled away.

Any other day, Jessie would have sat on the dock to examine the contents of the pouch, but today she just hurriedly sorted through it. Captain Dave had put in a little bag of peppermint drops, but Jessie didn't feel like eating even one. There were two letters, one from her father and the other from Helen. She would take them to her mother as soon as she sent off the letter, the one she *hadn't* put in the pouch for the mailboat.

Jessie hurried down the beach until she was out of sight of even the very top of the lighthouse. Then she took the red bandana off the basket she was carrying and lifted out one of her mother's canning jars. Inside the green-tinted glass was the letter from her mother to the Lighthouse Service. With trembling hands, Jessie tightened the lid. Then, with all her strength, she threw the jar as far as she could out into the water.

She watched for a minute as it bobbed up and down on the waves. Turning to pick up her basket and the mail pouch, her eyes caught a movement in the clump of cottonwood trees. It was Omie hobbling toward her. Had Omie seen her throw the jar? Jessie gathered up her things and ran down the beach toward the lighthouse.

She was out of breath by the time she passed the fog signal building. A stone turned as she stepped on it, and she fell, wincing as her blistered hands struck the stony beach.

Jessie cried from the burning pain in her hands, but then she cried harder, not for her hands, but for what she had just done with her mother's letter. Last night she had tossed and turned in her bed when she thought about what she was going to do. This morning she had forced herself not to think about it. Just do it, get it over with, she had told herself.

At the top of the lighthouse, Jessie's mother was climbing down the ladder. She had just finished cleaning the tall panes that surrounded the light. Looking down, she saw her daughter sprawled on the beach.

"Jessie!" she shouted. "Are you all right?"

Gathering up the basket and the mail pouch, Jessie scrambled to her feet. "I'm fine, Mama. I just turned my ankle. I'm all right."

"Did you mail the letters?" her mother called down.

"I mailed them, Mama," Jessie said dabbing her bleeding fingers with the bandana that had covered the basket. Three lies in less than a minute, she thought as she blinked back her tears.

She looked up at her mother, up so high, her black skirt billowing out around her. "Be careful, Mama." Jessie half-prayed, half-spoke the words into the wind that was blowing from the northwest.

She felt a sudden chill. In her mind, she saw the ice piled in great chunks on the beach, the ice shrouding the lighthouse. November, she thought, was only three weeks away. November, the worst month on the lake, when storms churned up mountainous waves, and ice and snow seemed to come from every direction at once. Jessie pressed the bandana hard between her blistered, bleeding hands.

Winter. The word sent a chill down her spine. There had never been a winter as bad as the last one. Before the shipping season ended, more than two hundred sailing men had lost their lives.

Maybe her mother was right. Maybe they did need help. Maybe the two of them couldn't keep the light going by themselves. What if something happened to Mama? Could she, Jessie, see herself up on that icy, narrow balcony in the middle of the night? Could she see herself scraping the ice off the windows so the light could shine out across the Manitou Passage? Jessie's mouth went dry and she swallowed hard.

"Maybe there won't be any storms in November. Maybe Papa will come home early," she said out loud to herself. A seagull wheeled, screeching around her. It sounded like a cruel laugh. Out on the lake, the gull settled itself on the water, a speck of white bobbing up and down on the waves, and Jessie thought about her mother's letter, the letter the Lighthouse Service would probably never get.

11

Jessie pushed her half-eaten dinner of fried potatoes aside and glanced again at Helen's letter. Her sister had taken a whole page to describe how she was helping Miss Pym teach the alphabet to the new students. Jessie barely looked at Miss Pym's neatly written page of school assignments that Helen had enclosed in her letter.

Jessie's mother smiled as she folded the letter from her husband. "Your father said to give you his love, Jessie, and to tell you he's right on schedule, which means he should be home around the middle of November."

"The middle of November? I—I thought he'd be home earlier than that," Jessie stammered.

"Well, you know, Jessie, everything depends on the weather. If the sun shines, if there are no storms or fog, he might be back sooner. And when he gets my letter I know he'll try to come home as soon as he can. But if no captain can take his place, or if there is bad weather . . ." Her voice trailed off. "Jessie, I'm glad we sent those letters. I know you didn't want me to send the one to the Lighthouse Service, but what if something happened to me? We need help."

Jessie wanted to tell her mother what she had done, but the words got all choked up together in her throat. Instead she burst into tears. "Nothing is going to happen to you, Mama," she sobbed.

"Jessie, Jessie," her mother said, cupping Jessie's cold hands in her warm ones. "I didn't mean to scare you. Nothing is going to happen to me. Don't worry."

Jessie thought of her mother's letter bobbing up and down in its jar of a mailboat somewhere out in Lake Michigan, and she couldn't stop crying.

"What's wrong, Jessie?" Her mother's voice, which used to comfort her more than anything else, now made Jessie cry only harder.

Jessie wanted to tell her, tell her what she'd done with the letter. Instead, she said, "I miss Papa." She wondered if, from now on, everything that came out of her mouth would be only half the truth. "I want you to teach me everything about the light, Mama," Jessie said, so suddenly and with such seriousness that her mother looked at her in surprise.

"Everything?" she asked.

Jessie felt her mother's eyes measuring her, just as Granddad's had.

"Yes, Mama, everything," she said. In her mind she pictured herself up on the narrow iron balcony, and she felt sick.

As the days of October slipped by, Jessie did the schoolwork that Miss Pym had assigned. She also followed her mother on her lightkeeping duties, asking questions and learning how to do everything that needed to be done to keep the light burning. Now she was able to light the lamp. She could raise the three wicks just high enough and then lower them quickly so they didn't smoke. She learned how to cover their circles of flame with the glass chimney and how to put on the damper. When all was ready, she opened the door of the great lantern and set the lamp carefully inside.

She had helped her mother fix the chain on the fog bell. In a notebook, Jessie wrote down directions for everything, so she would know what to do if for some reason, a reason too awful to think about, her mother wasn't able to help her.

But there was one thing Jessie couldn't do, couldn't make herself do, and that was to go out onto the balcony that circled the top of the lighthouse. Jessie recalled the time, just after her grandfather died, when her mother had asked her to hold the ladder so she could climb up to the top balcony to wash the panes of glass. She remembered her mother lugging the wooden ladder out the iron door and onto the lower balcony, lifting those small iron hooks over the short, flimsy-looking railing above. She remembered her mother, still reeling from Granddad's death, her face swollen from crying and her hands trembling. Her mother had needed her to steady the ladder, and she had failed her.

Her mother had warned, "Don't look down, Jessie. Look straight out. Look at the mainland. Look at the clouds. You don't have to look down."

But Jessie hadn't been able to help herself. Her eyes, her whole body had seemed to be pulled toward the roof of the house far below. The lighthouse had seemed to be spinning, and then she had gotten sick. She had crawled back into the lighthouse, shaking and whimpering like a scared puppy.

Since that time, the closest Jessie had come to being outside on the balcony was when she was up in the lantern room. Up in this topmost part of the lighthouse, the windows stretched from the black metal floor all the way to the ceiling. When Jessie was up there cleaning the curved glass pieces of the lantern, she couldn't bring herself to look at her mother, out on the other side of the glass, busily polishing the windows, her mother out on that narrow metal balcony with the low railing, low so that it didn't obstruct the light.

When her mother climbed down the outside ladder to the

wider balcony below, Jessie squeezed her eyes shut and fought the panic that rose up in her like a big wave. She couldn't even make herself go onto that lower balcony, where at least there was a railing as high as her waist.

As long as Jessie imagined that she was totally enclosed, totally encircled by the strong brick walls, she could handle her fear. In front of her mother, Jessie tried to act as if it were the most natural thing in the world for her to be up at the top of the lighthouse, but her hands were so sweaty she had to keep wiping them on her skirt.

Jessie hadn't seen Omie since the day she had thrown the jar with her mother's letter in it into Lake Michigan. Had Omie watched her do it? Omie usually came around the house a few times a month. Her mother always had a basket of food set aside for her. Where was Omie?

"Maybe she's dead," Jessie said to herself and was shocked to realize that she would be glad if that were true.

12

As Jessie scrubbed the breakfast dishes, she said a prayer that she must have prayed a thousand times since the day the jar with her mother's letter in it hit the water. She prayed that her mother would stay strong and healthy, the good weather would hold, and there would be no storms, at least not until her father came home. Last night she had had a terrible dream. A wall of water, a tidal wave, had knocked the lighthouse off its foundation and swept them—

"Jessie!" Her mother's voice broke through her thoughts. "Is there something wrong? I've been calling your name and you haven't heard me." She stirred another spoonful of sugar into her tea and said, "You've been doing that a lot lately, honey. Are you not feeling well?"

The heavy platter Jessie was washing slipped out of her hands and fell back into the wash basin sending water cascading over the side. She was so tired of all the lies she had told. She wanted to throw her arms around her mother and tell her what she had done with the letter. But when she opened her mouth, the words wouldn't come out. Instead she said, "Oh, I guess I'm worried. I mean, I'm just tired."

Rubbing her forehead, her mother sighed. "I guess that makes two of us tired and worried. I don't know why we haven't heard anything from the Lighthouse Service. They know the storms are only a few weeks, if not a few days, away. I thought surely there would be a letter in yesterday's mail."

Jessie turned back to her scrubbing. From the warmth that rose up in her face, she knew it was red. A tear rolled down her cheek and into the soapy water. She could hardly remember what it felt like to be able to say what she really wanted to say, to just tell the truth without having to think about every word.

Stiffly getting up from the table, her mother straightened herself up. Brushing aside the window curtains, she looked out. "Oh, dear," she said, "the wind's picked up and I left my polishing cloth tied to the railing. It's my best one. I don't want to lose it." She rearranged the curtains and, turning to Jessie, added, "But I'm just too tired to go back up right now."

Jessie wondered if maybe, just maybe, her mother had left the cloth tied to the balcony's railing on purpose, as a test. No, her mother wouldn't do that. Her mother wouldn't think of doing something like that. She looked at the dark shadows under her mother's eyes and noticed for the first time how thin her face had become.

"I'll get the cloth, Mama. You rest," she said, drying her shaking hands on the towel.

Her mother came over to where Jessie was standing and, putting her arms around her, assured her, "You don't have to do it if you don't think you can, Jessie. It's my job to be outside up there."

"I'll get the polishing cloth, Mama. I said I would." Jessie tried to keep her voice from shaking.

Her mother kissed her on the cheek. Then, drawing her shawl tighter around her shoulders, she made her way up the steps to her bedroom.

Jessie kicked the black iron leg of the cookstove. A sharp pain shot through her big toe. Tears rolled down her cheeks. "I'm crying because my toe hurts," she told herself.

13

Jessie's footsteps clanged on the metal steps as she climbed round and round to the top of the lighthouse. Halfway up, her long skirt tangled around her legs and she fell forward against the next sharp step. A dull pain shot through her right leg. Her hands on the iron handrail were cold and sweaty. Round and round she walked, slower and slower up the curving steps.

As she cleared the second hatch, she was almost knocked backward by a strong gust of wind that blew in through the open iron door. Jessie dropped to her knees and crawled over to the opening. Looking out along the lower balcony, she couldn't see the white cloth. Maybe it's already blown off, she thought. But turning her head, she caught sight of it fluttering from the railing of the narrow, scary balcony above her.

"I can't, I can't do it, " she said holding onto the metal door. Hadn't she gotten dizzy and sick just being out on the lower balcony, where at least the railing was higher and where strong bars were spaced every foot?

Then she remembered her bold words to her mother just a few weeks ago: "We can keep the light, Mama, just the two of us. We don't need any help." And in her mind she could see herself throwing the jar with her mother's letter in it into the blue waters of Lake Michigan. "We don't need any help, we don't need any help," her words taunted her.

Taking a deep breath, Jessie crawled out onto the smooth metal floor of the balcony. She kept her eyes focused on the place where the black metal met the curving, white wall of the lighthouse and made her way to the wooden ladder propped against the wall.

"God, help me. Please, help me," she prayed. She grabbed the rungs of the ladder and began her climb. The wind tore at her skirt as she stepped over the top of the ladder and down onto the upper balcony. Up here there was no white wall to lean against. There were just the tall windows that surrounded the lantern.

Jessie was almost overcome by the light, the airiness. She looked out across the water, which was tan near the shore, then turquoise, then deep blue. She stared across to the low, forested hills of the mainland that looked almost as blue as the water. "Just don't look down, Jessie. Don't look down," she told herself.

Up here, the railing was barely as high as her knees and the bars of the railing were so far apart that even a large man could slip through. Is that what had happened to Uncle Jim? He had died in a terrible accident, Jessie knew. But no one would ever tell her what happened.

"Don't think about that, Jessie. Not now," she said out loud. But it was too late. Jessie's whole body began to shake so violently that the only thing she could do was to lie down on the narrow metal balcony and press her forehead into the bumpy metal floor. The fingers of her left hand clenched the sharp edge of the metal, which seemed to hang like a thin plate over nothingness. Waves of nausea swept over her.

Finally she raised her head. She could see the white polishing cloth fluttering from the railing a few feet ahead of her. Inching her way along on her stomach, she reached the cloth. Then she turned over onto her back and worked at the knot until it came loose. She tucked the cloth into her pocket and crawled back toward the ladder. Suddenly she realized she would have to stand and step backward onto the rungs of the ladder to get down.

Dark clouds had boiled up out of nowhere. A streak of lightning hit the waters of the lake, which had quickly turned as gray as the pointed slate roof of the house far below.

14

Jessie couldn't stop herself from staring down. There on the beach, seeming so small from up so high, was a dark figure. It was Omie. The old woman looked up, and Jessie imagined she could hear the familiar chant, *"Alle fallen down, alle fallen down."*

Lightning streaked across the sky again, and the lighthouse shook as the thunder rolled. Jessie peered at the ladder hooked onto the railing above her.

"God, help me," she prayed again. She wiped her face on her sleeve and rubbed her wet hands on her skirt. Then she got to her knees. She would have to stand up straight in this place of lightning and wind with the seagulls reeling and screeching around her.

Jessie swallowed hard and leaned into the glass, her arms outstretched. She inched her way up until she was standing. She could feel the tower swaying ever so slightly in the wind. With fumbling hands, she reached behind herself for the place where the ladder was hooked to the railing. Holding on so tightly that her fingernails cut into the wood, she stepped over the railing and onto the top rung of the ladder, first one foot, then the other, telling herself not to look down, not to look down. Slowly she descended the rungs. When her foot hit the metal floor of the lower balcony, she dropped to her knees and crawled over to the safety of the open doorway.

Inside the lighthouse, Jessie felt numb. Chilled and shaking, she pressed her back against the strong, curving wall. She felt as weak as she had last winter, when she had been sick for days with a burning fever.

Taking the polishing cloth from her pocket, she smoothed it out on her lap. She had done it. She had gone out onto the lower balcony by herself and climbed the ladder to the upper one. No one needed to know how frightened she had been.

"If it *was* a test," Jessie said, looking at the cloth, "I passed it."

Clutching her trophy, Jessie hurried down the winding steps of the lighthouse. As she passed the windows in the watch room, she glanced out. Rain spattered against the glass. Jessie spotted Omie below, making her way up the path to the house. In her hands she carried a jar—with something in it.

"Omie! Omie!" Jessie yelled, beating on the windowpane. But there was no way Omie could hear.

A clap of thunder shook the lighthouse as Jessie tore down the steps. Racing through the passageway that connected the light to the house, she arrived at the door to the kitchen just in time to see her mother open the outside door for Omie.

"Omie!" Jessie cried.

Startled, the old woman dropped the jar. It smashed into pieces on the stone step.

"Jessie," her mother said. "Look what you made Omie do."

Turning to collect the shards of glass, her mother saw the white envelope sticking out of the broken jar. She picked it up and turned it over, staring at the letter she had sent weeks before to the Lighthouse Service.

"Omie. Where did you find this?" she asked.

Omie smiled her toothless smile. "*In der lake,*" she said, looking very pleased with herself.

Jessie edged back toward the passageway to the lighthouse,

crumpling the polishing cloth in her hands as the expression on her mother's face turned from disbelief to anger.

"Please excuse us, Omie," she said. "Come sit at the table and have a cup of tea." Then she motioned for Jessie to follow her into the sitting room and closed the door.

She whirled around, her face red with anger. "You did this," she said, her voice almost choking on the words. "Jessie Lafferty, how could you?"

15

Just as the winds of the storm swept the remaining leaves from the trees, the wind that blew almost constantly now from the northwest swept before it the warm days. Even if the sun shone, there was a chill in the air. When Jessie came in from feeding the chickens, her cheeks and hands were freezing cold. Though she had apologized over and over for not sending the letter and her mother said that she had forgiven her, things had changed between the two of them. Her mother had trusted her, and Jessie had betrayed that trust. Would she ever earn it back? Jessie felt a hollowness inside her, an emptiness she didn't know how to begin to fill. And she knew that her mother worried, constantly, going outside and looking anxiously at the lake whenever the sky darkened.

Jessie had had plenty of time to think about what it meant for no one to know they needed help. The twice-a-month mailboat that could have carried a second letter to the Lighthouse Service had come and gone the day before Omie arrived with the canning jar. If anything happened to her mother, what would she do? She couldn't tend the light by herself. Yes, she had gone up onto the upper balcony, but it had been daylight and she had shaken with fear.

She prayed that her mother would stay healthy. She prayed that her father would come home early. She prayed that the lake would stay calm and the skies clear, but none of her praying could stop the marching of the days toward winter. And Jessie knew that soon the storms would come.

On the seventh day of November, she found ice on the bucket of water that stood by the well. To try to get the sight, the feel, of that cold, transparent disk out of her thoughts, she set to work cooking something more complicated than usual for their noontime meal, something that would please her mother. And, because she put her whole mind to it, for once she didn't burn anything.

"Jessie, your colcannon was delicious," her mother said, bringing her empty plate over to Jessie to wash. The dish was Irish and one of her mother's favorites. Jessie had made it well, carefully cooking the onions, cabbage, and carrots until they were soft and mashing the potatoes till all the lumps were out.

As Jessie scrubbed the skillet, her mother took her basket out of the cupboard and began tucking various items, a bag of coffee beans and tins of sugar and cocoa, into it. Turning to Jessie, she said, "I'd like you to pay a quick visit to the Hostetlers today, honey. We haven't seen either of them for a while, and I want to be sure they're both all right."

"Stubborn," Granddad had always said about Mr. Hostetler and his ways.

"Independent," her mother had always corrected him. And teasing, she had always added, "And you're just like him."

"Couldn't I go tomorrow instead?" Jessie asked, pumping water into the basin to rinse the dishes. Like her mother, Jessie felt uneasy with each change of weather. And since morning the wind had picked up. Now it was blowing strongly from the northwest.

"There was ice this morning up on the light," her mother said. "And it feels even colder now. I might need you here tomorrow, Jessie."

Jessie hung the dish towel and her apron on their pegs and grabbed her shawl off the chair. "I'll go right now, Mama." If she had to go, she wanted to have enough time to get back while there was still plenty of daylight. Darkness came earlier and earlier these November days.

"Thank you, Jessie," her mother said, giving her a quick smile. "Tell the Hostetlers if they need any kerosene, we have extra. You can take that over some other day." She pried the lid off a tin of Granddad's tobacco, smelled it, and quickly replacing the lid, put the tobacco into the basket, too.

Jessie barely heard her mother. In her mind, she was tracing the route she didn't like to walk alone, the narrow, sandy road that ran straight across the island, past the cemetery's white crosses, and on through the Hostetlers' patch of woods where the noises were so different from those here on the shore.

"You might come across Omie on your way."

The name *Omie* brought Jessie to attention.

"If you see her, try to make her understand that she can come and stay with us now that it's turning cold. We certainly have room to spare."

"I don't want her living here with us," Jessie said, nervously twisting one of her braids.

"Jessie, that's so selfish!" her mother said. "Think of her in that falling-down shack and us here in this strong, warm house. Aren't we our brother's keeper?"

But Jessie wasn't in their warm kitchen with its starched red-and-white checked curtains, its cupboard with all the plates and cups neatly arranged. In her mind, she saw Omie in her black rags scuffling through their dark bedrooms muttering, *"Fallen down, alle fallen down."*

"She might kill us while we're sleeping!" Jessie blurted out.

Her mother's mouth dropped open. "Jessie! Why would that thought even enter your head?"

"I don't like her, Mama. I've never liked her. She smells. She doesn't have any teeth. She slobbers."

"Jessie, you know Omie's story. Years ago she was put ashore on this island, she and her little girl, as if they were animals nobody wanted. Now she's an old woman who has no one to help her except us and Mr. and Mrs. Hostetler. Omie never did anything to hurt anyone. Certainly she never hurt you. Well, did she, Jessie?"

"I don't know, Mama," Jessie said.

"If Omie ever hurt you, you'd remember. Now let that be the end of this nonsense."

Jessie was almost in tears, trying to sort out in her mind why she was so afraid. She knew it was more than Omie's uncouth manners and appearance. "I—I just can't remember, Mama."

"Jessie, isn't it about time you started thinking more about others and less about yourself?" her mother asked. Shaking her head and pursing her lips, she turned back to her work.

Jessie looked over at her mother, who was carefully covering the basket with one of her best linen towels. She knew her mother was beyond exhaustion. She used to stand so straight and tall, her hair caught back neatly in her favorite comb, but now her shoulders slumped and her hair trailed out of the long braid she had taken to wearing loose down her back. Jessie felt her mother's disappointment in her fill the room.

"I'm sorry, Mama," she said in a small voice.

Her mother turned and, going over to Jessie, put her arms around her. Quietly but firmly she said, "We both have to do things we don't want to do. To get through this, we have to, Jessie. You know that."

Jessie laid her head against her mother's shoulder. "I know, Mama. I know."

16

Even though the cold wind made her cheeks feel like ice, by the time Jessie reached the cemetery she was sweating and out of breath. No grass had grown on Granddad's grave. The seeds her mother had scattered lay parched in the dust, and the white cross had fallen over. Jessie set down her basket and pushed the cross's pointed end into the sandy dirt.

She could picture Granddad's face so clearly. "Oh, Granddad," she whispered, wiping the tears off her cheeks with the end of her shawl. "We need your help."

She touched the cross that marked the grave of her Uncle Jim. What was the terrible accident no one would talk about? For a second, she felt as if she were standing on the white, frozen shore, looking up at the light, watching as her Uncle Jim turned to look down at her . . .

Jessie was so caught up in her own thoughts that she didn't hear Omie behind her. Backing away from the graves, she almost fell over the old woman, who was bending down to look in her basket.

"*Fallen down, fallen down,*" she muttered and reached for the tin of sugar.

"No, Omie!" Jessie said. "These things are for the Hostetlers. You can't have them."

The hurt look on the old woman's face cut Jessie to the

quick. Hadn't she just promised her mother she would try to think about other people's needs?

"I'm sorry, Omie," she said. "If I could give you some of these, I would. You know my mother always has a basket ready for you. Just go to the house. All right?"

Omie nodded and gave Jessie a toothless smile. *"Jessie, meine Jessie,"* she said. Lifting her ragged shawl to cover her head, she shuffled down the road toward the lighthouse, the hems of her clothes dragging in the dust.

Jessie rearranged the towel over the basket and quickened her pace down the sandy road toward the Hostetlers'. The sky was getting darker by the minute. Not until the old woman was out of sight did Jessie remember her mother's request to invite Omie to stay with them. Although the thought of Omie wandering around in their house at night still made Jessie shudder, she promised herself she would relay the message the very next time she saw her. But Mama will see her this afternoon, she thought. She'll tell her.

Omie's words *"fallen down"* echoed in Jessie's ears. She had the feeling it was a puzzle, a riddle she could almost figure out. It was like a dream she had just before waking, a dream that was so vivid she felt she could almost experience it again . . . but always, always, it was just out of reach.

17

"My land," Mrs. Hostetler said when she opened the door to Jessie's knock, "aren't you a sight for sore eyes! Come in." She ushered Jessie into the warm kitchen that always smelled like freshly baked bread. "It's been a day for visitors."

Taking the basket Jessie held out to her, she said, "Now, now, your mother doesn't always need to send a basket of goodies to us old people. But we do appreciate everything, the thoughtfulness, and seeing your sweet little face." As was her custom, she kissed Jessie on both cheeks and gently pinched her nose. "Yes, Omie was here earlier, just wandering around outside. I couldn't get her to come in, but you know how old Rolf growls at her."

Rolf, the Hostetlers' collie, was wagging his tail so hard that his whole body wagged back and forth. Jessie knelt to scratch his ears and pet his silky back.

"A good afternoon to you, Miss Jessie," white-haired Mr. Hostetler said from his rocking chair by the fire. "Come sit over here. Warm yourself, child," he said and motioned to the chair opposite him. Jessie had always thought the Hostetlers' large farmhouse kitchen was the most comfortable room in the world.

"You know Omie has been acting more strangely than usual lately," Mrs. Hostetler said, tying a clean white apron over her skirt.

"If that's possible," Mr. Hostetler said, placing the book he'd been reading on the table beside his chair.

"Oh, the poor woman," Mrs. Hostetler said as she fussed about cutting slices of warm bread. "To think that someone—how many years ago was that Mr. Hostetler?—would just abandon her, with a young child, no less, here on this island." She slathered the pieces of bread with butter. "Heaven knows, we've done what we could to help her, and so has your mother, Jessie. But a person has to accept the help that's offered."

"And she's not able to do that," Mr. Hostetler cut in.

"That's not her fault, " Mrs. Hostetler added. "Peach butter, Jessie?" she asked. At Jessie's quick, "Yes, please," she spooned her golden preserves onto the bread and arranged the slices on a plate, the blue willow one she knew Jessie liked.

"Thank you, ma'am," Jessie said, reminding herself to be ladylike and not just gobble the bread, as she wanted to, in a few large bites.

"You're very welcome," Mrs. Hostetler said, stirring the cocoa that was coming to a boil on the stove. "If I remember right, Omie wasn't nearly in such a world of her own when her little girl was living. They never did find the child's body. The poor little thing just walked out onto the ice and disappeared. Sometimes I think Omie is still looking for her, expecting to find her still alive somewhere on this island. *Jessie* was her name, too. Did you know that, Jessie?"

"Yes, ma'am, I think my mother told me a long time ago," Jessie replied, starting on her second slice of bread.

Mrs. Hostetler put a tray of three steaming cups on the table beside Jessie. "Here, let's put some cream in this cocoa to cool it down a bit," she said.

The heat in the kitchen, the warm bread, Mrs. Hostetler's chatter, and the smell of the cocoa had almost lulled Jessie to sleep. This is the way things used to be at our house, Jessie thought, especially when Grandma was alive—apple pies, cinnamon rolls, pans of gingerbread. Was I eight or nine when she died?

Mr. Hostetler's deep voice interrupted her daydream. "How are you getting along down there at the lighthouse?"

"All right, sir," Jessie mumbled. It was a relief to Jessie that at least the Hostetlers knew about Granddad's death. Even though almost the whole three-mile width of the island lay between their farm and the lighthouse, it was comforting to think of them as neighbors. Five and a half weeks ago, Mr. Hostetler had helped bury Granddad.

The elderly man took his pipe out of his pocket. Removing the lid from his tin of tobacco, he scooped up the dry, sweet-smelling leaves and began tapping them into the pipe's wooden bowl. "Well, Jessie," he said, "it's not as if your family hasn't had its share of tragedies there at the lighthouse. What with Jim's accident—"

"We don't need to dwell on sad things," Mrs. Hostetler interrupted. "Here, Jessie, have some more cocoa."

Jessie was drinking the last of her second cup when Mr. Hostetler asked, "Who did the Lighthouse Service send to help your mother tend the light?"

Jessie's throat tightened and she started to cough. "No one yet."

"What?" Mr. Hostetler set his pipe down so hard on the arm of his chair that the tobacco spilled out of the bowl.

"I can't believe that. How irresponsible can those people be?"

Jessie wished now she had never come. She didn't know what to say. She couldn't tell the Hostetlers what she had done with her mother's letter. "I'm—I'm helping her," she said, covering her chin with her hand to hide its quivering.

"Jessie, I'm not trying to upset you," Mr. Hostetler said. "No one on God's good earth could have done a better job than your family. And I'd hate to see the lighthouse given over to someone else. But, girl, you and your mother can't manage it alone. What would you do if something happened to her?"

"Nothing's going to happen to my mother," Jessie said, clenching her fists so hard her fingernails dug into her skin. She would not let herself cry. "We're getting along just fine."

"You're spunky, Jessie," Mr. Hostetler said, "But you're a young girl, and you're slight. It's a wonder the wind doesn't blow you away. I'm sure you're a help in the house with the cooking and all—but I mean up at the top of the lighthouse."

"I've been up on the upper balcony by myself. I didn't get blown off," Jessie said, trying to blink back the tears that kept welling up in her eyes.

The old man got up out of his chair so quickly that it was left rocking by itself. "A girl your age has no business on that God-forsaken upper balcony!" he almost shouted.

"Now, of course you're a help to your mother," Mrs. Hostetler said, giving her husband a sharp look.

Mr. Hostetler closed his mouth as if to keep in all the other things he wanted to say about the Service leaving a woman and child to tend one of the most important lighthouses on Lake Michigan during the stormiest month of the year.

"I'm going to check the animals," he said. "Bad weather's coming."

Jessie saw the concerned glance the two exchanged before he went out the door. She ran to look out Mrs. Hostetler's white-curtained window. Though it was mid-afternoon, the sky was dark with storm clouds.

"Why don't you wait awhile, Jessie, and Mr. Hostetler will walk back to the lighthouse with you," Mrs. Hostetler said, hurriedly repacking Jessie's basket with jars of jelly and one of her freshly baked loaves of bread.

But Jessie's stomach had turned into a knot. "I'd better start back right now," she said. "Do you think it'll be bad?"

As if in answer, the kitchen door blew open and a cold rain pelted in.

18

The wind tore at the rain cape Mrs. Hostetler insisted Jessie take and keep. It seemed that for every two steps she took, the wind pushed her back one.

Now the stand of giant cedars loomed ahead of her. The branches of the stringy-barked trees whipped back and forth. She thought about retracing her steps and making her way along the shoreline, but that would take longer. Pulling the rain cape tighter around her neck, she started to run through the twisting, turning branches.

"I have to get back to the lighthouse. I have to get back." Jessie said the words out loud as if saying them would help her get there quicker. She had a sense that something was wrong, terribly wrong there.

A bolt of lightning sliced into a tree nearby. Half the trunk crashed across the narrow, sandy road. The wood smoked, filling the air with the acrid smell of burning pine. When she tried to walk around the fallen tree, its branches grabbed at her cape. Finally, climbing, scrambling over them, she was back on the road.

At the cemetery, a gust of wind blew the cape's hood off her head, and she set her basket down to retie it. Thunder cracked again. The wind changed direction. It was spitting rain, cold rain.

From the stand of cedars came a distant moan, the wind playing the branches like an instrument.

Jessie grabbed her basket and started at a half-run down the road to the light. The cape and her long skirt kept tangling around her legs. Her mind jumped from one terrible image to another, her mother lying on the rocks below the lighthouse, her mother caught in an undertow of waves, her mother—and there, in front of her on the road, was Omie.

When Jessie saw the tin of sugar clutched in her hands, she knew that Omie had been to the lighthouse and had seen her mother.

"Is my mother all right? Is she safe?" Jessie asked, bending down to look into Omie's filmy eyes.

"Da Mudder all right?" Omie repeated Jessie's question.

"Omie," Jessie tried again, this time speaking more slowly, as if that might help the words sink in. "Is my mother safe? I'll give you Mrs. Hostetler's bread and jellies if you answer me."

Omie shook her head back and forth. *"Alle fallen down,"* she said.

"Did my mother fall?"

"Nein, nein," Omie said.

Jessie set the basket at Omie's feet. Tearing off the cumbersome rain cape, she started to run toward the lighthouse. Then, remembering Omie, she yelled back, "Thank you, Omie! Thank you!" The old woman had already ripped off a piece of bread and was stuffing it into her mouth. She stopped and waved the rest of the loaf at Jessie.

Suddenly Jessie was aware of the fog bell clanging its warning. Had it just started? She wasn't sure. It might have been ringing for a long time and she had been so frantic with worry that she hadn't noticed.

"I'm not far from home," she told herself as she ran down the path that cut through the patch of scrubby pines that stood between her and the beach. The sound of the bell was all mixed up with her fears. She tried to think. If the fog bell had just started ringing, her mother would have started it. That would mean she was all right.

Jessie stumbled out onto the beach. The light, the strong, beautiful, white candle of the lighthouse, loomed up from its rocky base. The lantern burned brightly through the gathering darkness and the fog bell clanged. Breathing a sigh of relief, she slowed her pace to a walk. "Everything is fine." She whispered the words as if they were a prayer.

Jessie turned up the path that led around the house to the kitchen and saw the crumpled form of her mother lying on the steps.

19

"Mama!" In an instant Jessie was on the steps bending over her. Her mother raised her head.

"Mama, what happened?" Jessie touched her mother's shoulder and peered anxiously into her face.

Her mother struggled to sit up. "The steps were wet. I was in too big of a hurry."

Jessie tried to help her to her feet, but her mother winced with every movement.

"How can I help you without hurting you, Mama?" Jessie cried.

Lightning zigzagged into the dark waters of the lake. The clap of thunder was instantaneous and deafening. Just as the wind shifted, from around the corner of the house came Omie. Wearing the cape Jessie had discarded, she swung the basket filled with Mrs. Hostetler's jellies back and forth.

Jessie's mother held out her hands to the old woman. "Please, Omie, would you help us?"

Omie stopped, put her basket on the ground, and lumbered up the steps.

"Alle fallen down, alle fallen down," she said.

"Mama, I can't stand her saying that all the time!" Jessie cried. Then felt her face turn hot. Here she was whining while her mother was hurt, maybe badly hurt.

Her mother didn't even reply with a scolding, as she normally would have. She already had her right hand in the crook of Omie's arm. With her left hand in Jessie's, she managed to rise to her feet. But when she put her weight on her right foot, she cried out in pain. Omie reached her arm around her mother's waist, and, with Omie bearing most of her mother's weight, the two helped her into the house.

Jessie was surprised at Omie's strength, but she knew there was no way they could get her mother up the narrow steps to her bedroom. "Let's go into the sitting room," she said.

After they maneuvered Jessie's mother onto the divan, Jessie hurried to light the kerosene lamp. Her hands were shaking so badly, the flame smoked the chimney. No time to take it off and clean it. Not now.

As Jessie worked to unfasten her mother's shoe, she could see the knuckles of her mother's hands whiten as she clenched her hands against the pain. When she gently rolled down her mother's dark stocking, Jessie was shocked at how purple and swollen the ankle looked.

"Just let me rest it for a while on a pillow," her mother said, trying to manage a smile. "I'll be fine, honey." She reached up to touch Jessie's face. "Go make some tea and give Omie something to eat."

Jessie didn't trust herself to say anything. Instead, she covered her mother with an afghan and kissed her on the cheek.

Jessie was more careful lighting the kitchen's kerosene lamp. But when she lifted the lamp onto the shelf above the table, her trembling almost rattled the chimney loose. Omie wandered restlessly back and forth between the kitchen and the sitting room. Jessie thought she smelled like a dirty, wet rug.

The water on the cookstove finally boiled. By the time the tea was ready, Omie had made herself at home, sitting in Jessie's chair at the kitchen table. Jessie poured Omie some tea and watched as the old woman spilled the hot brew into the saucer, blew on it, and began to slurp it.

Above a boom of thunder that rattled the house, Jessie heard her mother's voice calling her. Entering the sitting room, she found her mother trying to stand. "Oh, Mama," Jessie said.

Even though her mother's eyes were squinted shut, tears trickled out of the corners, wetting her cheeks. "Help me, Jessie," she said. "I don't think any bones are broken. I can walk." With her arm around Jessie's shoulders, she took a step with her good foot. But taking one step on her swollen right foot, she fell to the floor.

"Alle fallen down, alle fallen down," Omie said, looking in from the doorway.

It was all Jessie could do to keep from screaming at the old woman. She wanted to pound those words out of her with her fists. Instead, she helped her mother up and hugged her tight, her tears dampening her mother's hair.

20

It was a fact. Jessie's mother couldn't walk. Not now. Maybe not for weeks. It was another fact that Jessie couldn't stop the storm, the high waves, and the blasts of wind and sleet from coming.

Jessie cranked the handle of the fog bell. She had to think. She had to force herself to think. Everything depended on her now. Everything. The light, the bell, her mother, all the ships entering the Manitou Passage tonight. Jessie gripped the wooden handle tightly, winding, winding.

It was pitch dark outside. Night had come early. The metal gears of the fog bell reflected the light of Jessie's lantern. With a creak, the door swung open. Jessie turned her head to see Omie rocking back and forth in the doorway.

Right now, I need help, Jessie thought. Considering her feelings toward Omie, Jessie felt like a hypocrite, but if Omie could help with the bell, that would be one less thing to worry about. "Omie, I need you!" Jessie yelled, trying to make her voice heard over the *clang*.

Omie grinned and nodded.

"When the bell slows down," Jessie yelled, "turn this crank to wind it up again. Do you understand?"

Omie grinned and nodded again.

Jessie wasn't sure if Omie understood, so she took her hand, sticky with jelly, and placed it on the handle. She helped Omie turn the crank a few times. Then Omie did it herself. The old woman looked up at Jessie, a questioning look in her heavy-lidded eyes.

"Good, that was good, Omie," Jessie said cupping her hands so Omie could hear.

Omie smiled. "Good, good," she repeated.

"Just don't wind it too tight," Jessie added, remembering Omie's strength. If the chain broke . . . Jessie didn't even finish the thought. It wouldn't break. "Not too tight," Jessie said again.

Jessie hurried to build a fire in the pot-bellied stove and pulled up her grandfather's chair for Omie to sit on. Omie had already found his can of chewing tobacco. She spit a brown plug of it onto the brick floor. Jessie handed her an empty can. She didn't wait for her to spit again. Instead, she yelled, "Omie, remember, don't wind it too tight!"

Omie nodded and grinned. A streak of tobacco juice dribbled out of one corner of her mouth.

Cold rain stung Jessie's cheeks as she made her way up the dark path to the house. "Please, God," she prayed out loud. "Don't let the chain break." Jessie wondered if it had been a good idea after all to ask Omie to wind the bell. The good thing, Jessie thought, is that she's out of the house. The idea of Omie wandering around in the house and the possibility that Omie might climb up the winding steps of the lighthouse made Jessie shudder. At least I'll know where Omie is, she thought.

Jessie looked up at the light that her mother had lit before she had fallen, before everything had changed. The light was burning, but—the light that should have been piercingly bright was blurred. Something was happening to the light!

21

Jessie rushed into the sitting room. "Mama, the light! There's something wrong!"

Her mother looked at her, puzzled. Jessie was shocked at how strained her mother's face looked. Propped up on a pillow, her ankle had swollen to twice its normal size.

"Yes? What is it?" her mother asked, shaking her head as if to clear it.

"The light's blurry, Mama."

Trying to sit up, Jessie's mother said, "Check the outside of the kitchen window. See if there's ice on it."

Jessie had never heard fear in her mother's voice—until now. As Jessie pushed up the window, a gust of freezing wind tore the curtain rod off its hooks. Leaning outside, she reached up to touch the panes of glass. They were cold, but they weren't covered with ice.

"No ice, just rain," Jessie hurried to report.

"Thank God," her mother said, lying back down. She looked so tired. Jessie wished she could just let her mother sleep, but she had to have answers.

"But, Mama, what do I do? The light isn't shining clear."

Her mother struggled up onto her elbows. "The windows around the lantern are probably steamed up," she said. "It's gotten so cold outside, and the lamp makes heat up there. Go up into the watch room and get the bottle of glycerine. You know where that is, don't you?"

"Yes, Mama," Jessie replied, picking up the afghan that had fallen to the floor.

"Pour some of the glycerine onto a clean cloth—there should be several up there. Then wipe the inside of the windows around the lantern. That usually keeps the glass from fogging up."

Jessie covered her mother with the afghan. Her mother winced when it touched her ankle. "Let's just leave the ankle uncovered, honey," she said, trying to smile.

Jessie wanted to be the one being covered up, comforted. Nothing like this was supposed to happen. "Mama," she began, "I'm sorry. I thought there wouldn't be any storms. I thought Papa might come home."

Her mother reached over and took her hand. "How many times have we been through this, Jessie? You know I've forgiven you. Right now we just have to do the best we can." Her voice caught as she tried to shift her foot to a more comfortable position. She looked up at Jessie with so much concern and worry that Jessie had to quickly look down at the braided rug. Squeezing her daughter's hand, she corrected herself. "You'll have to do the best *you* can, Jessie."

A blast of cold air swept across the room. Jessie raced to close the kitchen window that in her haste she had left open.

Jessie struggled up the spiral steps of the lighthouse. The heavy oilcan banged against each iron step.

"One, two, three, four, five, . . ." she counted, her long skirt tangling around her legs. Every time she got to twenty-five she could rest on the small, level space before the next set of steps. On her next trip down, she vowed to find her grandfather's trousers and pull them on over her skirt. Maybe she would even wear his jacket instead of the shawl, which certainly wasn't designed for this kind of work.

She didn't have the strength to lift the oilcan up through the first hatch and onto the floor of the watch room. So, slowly, carefully, she backed down the last twenty-five steps. I'll just have to leave it down here, she thought, and make trips down to it when I need the oil.

In the watch room, she found the bottle of glycerine and the clean cloths. Tucking the cloths in the waistband of her skirt, she made her way up the final fourteen iron steps and lifted the second hatch. Quickly closing it, she climbed the ladder to the lantern.

Careful to avert her eyes from the blinding light, she poured some glycerine onto one of the cloths and began wiping the inside of the tall windows that surrounded the lantern. She moved quickly so she wouldn't obscure the light, so the ship captains could see that it was a steady light, the South Manitou Island Light, and not be confused.

Jessie didn't look down; she tried not even to look out. She tried to pretend that she was wiping the windowpanes in the kitchen, the windows that were nice and close to the ground. But she couldn't help feel the lighthouse swaying as it was blasted by the wind. Her hands were shaking so badly that she could hardly unfasten the brass latch on the lantern to check the oil in the lamp. She could see that it wouldn't last the whole night. She would have to get another lamp ready.

The glycerine seemed to be working. The big windows were no longer fogging up. Outside, the iron balcony gleamed shiny and wet. Jessie couldn't stop herself from looking. The railing seemed lower and flimsier than on that awful day she had climbed over it to get her mother's polishing cloth.

"You don't have to go out on the balcony, Jessie," she said to herself. "You don't have to do that."

Down in the watch room, she felt secure. The walls were thick and the windows were small. She felt too nervous to sit in the straight-backed chair her mother always used when she was watching the light. Instead, Jessie paced back and forth, the light from her lantern casting a curving shadow staircase on the wall. She looked out the windows for what must have been the hundredth time. Through the rain, through the storm, she watched the wind ripping the whitecaps off the waves.

Across the Manitou channel, on the mainland, Jessie knew the surf was pounding the base of the giant dune, the Sleeping Bear. The waves were washing over the dock at Leland, trying to rock the fishing boats loose from their moorings.

In the winter, when the shipping season was over, a thick sheet of ice would stretch across the channel. Jessie and her mother and father would join Helen in their grandparents' house there.

Jessie would be a student again in Leland's one-room schoolhouse. She hoped Miss Pym would read another book by Charles Dickens. At the end of every school day last year, the teacher had read aloud a chapter of *Oliver Twist*. How Jessie had looked forward to losing herself in that story. Losing herself in books caused Jessie the most trouble at school. Whenever she had gotten ahead in her lessons, she propped a book she'd brought from home inside her schoolbook. Before long, Miss Pym's voice would break through into the legend of King Arthur or the myth of Persephone or whatever else Jessie happened to be reading. The class would laugh as Jessie's face reddened, and she would find herself, once again, kept after school to sweep the floor or wash the slates. Despite that, she was one of Miss Pym's star pupils, second only to Lars Olsen in arithmetic and praised by everyone for her elocution. At special school programs, she had moved her grandmother and others in the audience to tears with her recitation of Henry Wadsworth Longfellow's poem "The Wreck of the Hesperus."

Jessie's father, who was used to cramped quarters from his life on ships, didn't mind the lack of space and privacy in the Leland house as much as Jessie's mother. It was, after all, his boyhood home. Reading biographies, preparing for the next shipping season, and helping with repairs to the house occupied his time throughout the long, dark months of winter.

Jessie's mother tried her best to be happy in the crowded house. In her rare spare time, she studied her book on rocks and fossils. Jessie's father had built her a special shelf for her collection, and it had a place of honor under the window of the sitting room of their island home. She had kept busy many an evening last winter, rubbing oil onto the coral fossils she found along the beach when no one else could, although they looked hard. The fossils were tumbled and polished smooth by the waves, but the oil brought out the patterns of the coral, more intricate than the finest needlework.

Mostly, though, she helped her mother-in-law with the cooking, sewing, and all the other household chores. As the snow deepened outside, everyone in the Leland house couldn't help but notice that she grew more and more quiet. Jessie knew that her mother was counting the days till she could return to the island in the spring. *Mama wants to keep the light as much as I do, probably more than I do,* Jessie thought. She knew that was the truth. Yet her mother had written that letter.

In her mind, for probably the hundredth time, Jessie saw again the canning jar with her mother's letter in it bobbing up and down on the waves. "I did it for you, Mama," Jessie found herself saying out loud to herself. The words sounded so hollow. The truth was something Jessie tried without success to push away, push down, bury. She hadn't done it for her mother. If she were truly honest, she would have to admit that she had done it for herself.

Jessie pressed her head against the cold wood of the window frame. A ship came into view, a schooner. Could it be her father's? By now, he would have gotten her mother's letter.

Then Jessie saw that the ship had only two masts, not the *Isabella*'s three. She watched the vessel pitch and toss as it headed for the crescent-shaped harbor of the island. As it took an especially deep plunge in the waves, Jessie's heart seemed to drop with it, and she prayed that her father was safe tonight, somewhere, in a sheltered port.

22

I'd better check on Mama—and Omie, Jessie thought. She still didn't trust Omie to wind the clock mechanism on the fog bell without breaking it.

Holding high the lantern, Jessie hurried down the steps of the lighthouse. Her skirt wound around her legs for what seemed like the hundredth time, and her heavy shawl kept slipping from her shoulders. "I think Granddad would want me to wear his clothes," she said.

The passageway was freezing cold, and the sitting room wasn't much warmer. By her mother's deep breathing, Jessie could tell that she was sound asleep. She didn't want to wake her by hauling in wood to make a fire. Gently, Jessie put another afghan on her, careful not to touch the ankle that looked even more swollen than before.

She tiptoed out of the room and up the stairs to her grandfather's bedroom. He had been wearing his old work clothes when he died, and her mother had buried him in his newer keeper's uniform, which he saved for the inspector's visits. Jessie found Granddad's older uniform in his closet, where he had last hung it. The jacket still smelled like him, of tobacco and damp wool. Jessie blinked back her tears as she struggled into the garment. Handkerchiefs on which she had embroidered his initials the Christmas before were crumpled in his pockets.

"Granddad, help me to be brave tonight," she prayed. She knew he was a saint somewhere up in heaven; she just hoped he was paying attention. As she stuffed her skirt into the trousers and rolled up the cuffs to make things fit, she prayed to God and everybody up there in heaven. Grandddad and Uncle Jim knew the light better than anyone else. She would depend especially on them.

She saw her grandfather's shoes in the bottom of the closet and decided to put them on, too. They were bigger than she thought they'd be, but by stuffing his handkerchiefs into each toe she made the shoes fit. Finally she wound her braids as best she could on top of her head and put on her grandfather's cap. In the glow of the lantern, she caught a glimpse of herself in the wavy glass of the mirror.

"I don't even look like me," she said, "but I don't look like Granddad either." She walked back and forth in the room to get used to the stiff shoes and the different, much freer way she could walk in trousers. Why didn't Mama think of this, she wondered.

The sound of sleet against the window beat into her thoughts. There had been a lull in the storm, but now it was starting up again. She grabbed the lantern and hurried down the stairs, still trying to be as quiet as she could. Outside, the sleet was now more snow than rain. The path to the fog-signal building was turning white. Jessie slid and almost fell.

As she opened the door, a gust of wind tore the handle from her hands. The door banged against the inside wall.

At the sound, Omie jerked awake. A look of terror spread across her face. "Jim!" she cried and hid her face in her hands.

Jessie whirled around, half expecting to see the ghost of Uncle Jim. But all she saw was the swirling snow. Then Jessie understood. "It's me—it's Jessie!" she shouted, trying to make herself heard over the sound of the bell. "I'm wearing Granddad's clothes."

Without taking her hands away from her face, Omie peered out between her fingers. Setting down the lantern, Jessie took off her grandfather's cap, releasing her braided hair.

Slowly, Omie uncovered her face. Frowning, she shook her head and, with the backs of her hands, wiped her eyes as if to clear them. *"Bad, Jessie. Bad, Omie. Fallen down, fallen down,"* she said, rocking back and forth. Fear and something like suspicion flitted over the old woman's features, but Jessie didn't have time to puzzle over them.

Turning her back on Omie, she grabbed the handle that wound the mechanism for the bell. "I'll wind it this time, Omie!" she yelled. Better that I do it than risk her breaking it, she thought, but there was another reason. She had to do something physical, something to still her pounding heart. She had felt safe and warm in Granddad's clothes, but Omie's cry and those words that Jessie wished she could erase from Omie's mind had ruined that.

When Jessie finished winding the bell, she put her grandfather's cap back on her head but, for Omie's sake, left her braids showing. "I'll be back to check that everything's all right, Omie!" she shouted.

As Jessie left the fog-signal building, Omie followed her as far as the doorway and stood there with the snow beginning to cling to her ragged clothes. Next time I come down, I'll bring her one of my shawls, Jessie thought. Could she hear Omie muttering to herself, *"Fallen, fallen,"* or did she just imagine it?

Halfway up the path, Jessie slid again and this time couldn't catch herself. Scrambling to her feet, she brushed herself off. "I'm fine!" she yelled back to the hulking figure silhouetted against the lamplight. "I'm fine," she repeated, more to reassure herself than Omie. The old woman shook her head and closed the door.

The waves were pounding the shore higher than Jessie had ever seen them. As she fought her way back toward the house, the sleet and snow came from every direction at once. Stopping to catch her breath, Jessie looked up at the light. It was dim again. It looked as if it were shining out through oiled paper instead of clear glass.

Back in the house, despite her attempt to be quiet, she couldn't manage to tiptoe in Granddad's shoes. Yet her mother slept on. Once Jessie reached the passageway, she didn't have to worry about how much noise she made, and this time, not having a heavy oilcan to lug up the steps, she made it to the lantern room in record time. As always, the light was blinding. Shielding her eyes, she grabbed the bottle of glycerine and a dry cloth and hurried to wipe the windows.

She rubbed, but nothing happened. She rubbed again and again, but none of her rubbing could wipe the white film away. The white was ice—ice on the outside of the lantern room.

"No!" Jessie screamed, and her cry echoed off the ice-shrouded windows.

23

Jessie hurried down the steps, stopping just long enough to clang shut the iron hatch doors. She clattered through the passageway and into the house.

"Mama, Mama!" she cried, but in the doorway to the sitting room she stopped. In the lamplight she could see that even though her mother still slept, lines of pain etched her face. Her ankle—Jessie took one look at her ankle and backed into the kitchen. It would do no good to waken her. She wasn't able to walk, let alone climb the steps of the lighthouse. And Jessie knew that if she wakened her, her mother would try to get up, that she would do anything she had to do to keep the light shining.

Jessie hurried down the kitchen steps into the blizzard outside. Looking up at the lighthouse, she could see the light was getting dimmer and dimmer as the ice glazed over the windows.

"I can't do it," Jessie said, clenching her fists to stop their shaking. "If I go up there, if I go outside up there, I'll fall. I know I will."

She wanted to curl up on the snow-covered ground and die. The full brunt of what she had done bore down on her with all the force of the north winds. Never had her family let the light fail, *never* until this night. And the shame of that swept over her like a giant wave.

Her mother's words echoed in her mind: "You'll have to do

the best you can, Jessie. You'll just have to do the best you can."

Out in the channel, a steamer blew long and low. The sound sliced like a knife into Jessie's thoughts. How many ships' captains were looking frantically for the light, praying for a lull in the blizzard so they could see the South Manitou Island Light? It was that image—the ships being tossed in the waves, the captains unable to see through the sheets of snow, the schooners with their sails growing heavy with ice—that finally made Jessie go back into the house.

"There's no one else," she told herself. "There's just no one else."

She knew where the ice scrapers were hung. Her grandfather had always kept them in the closet under the stairway. As a child, Jessie had never been allowed near them because their blades were so sharp.

She lifted the lantern to see into the darkness. The blades glowed like silver in the light. They had been newly sharpened. And Jessie knew that, while she had been praying that the ice storms would never come, her mother had been getting ready.

Halfway up the winding steps of the lighthouse, Jessie dropped one of the scrapers. It clanged against the steps as it fell. *"Fallen down, fallen down."* Omie's words echoed in her ears.

She retraced her steps round and round, down to the platform where the scraper had landed. Everything in her wanted to just keep going down, down the winding steps, away from the top of the lighthouse and what she would find there. But the ships, if she could just keep remembering the ships. Picking up the scraper, she hung it and its twin around her neck. There was a reason, other than for hanging them on a peg in the closet, for those long leather cords.

By the time Jessie pushed open the hatch and climbed up into the watch room, she was covered with sweat. Her grandfather's heavy wool jacket felt prickly through her cotton blouse.

"Please, God, make a hot wind," she prayed. "Please help the windows be clear of ice."

In the watch room she grabbed another cloth. Maybe the glass is just fogged up on the inside after all. Maybe I just didn't rub hard enough, she thought. She had always had trouble keeping her imagination under control. Maybe, once again, it was conjuring up a danger that didn't exist.

Slowly, she raised the hatch that led to the base of the light. Shielding her eyes, she looked up. In the dazzling light she couldn't tell if the windows were white from steam on the inside or ice on the outside.

Watching out for the sharp blades, Jessie carefully lifted the ice scrapers off her neck and placed them on the floor beside the bottle of glycerine. "Maybe I just didn't soak the cloth well enough," she said out loud. This time she took care to saturate the cloth and then slowly made her way up the ladder. She rubbed the inside of the windows until the glass was warm to the touch. But none of her rubbing had any effect on the opaque whiteness that surrounded the lantern like a white wall. And she knew, beyond any doubt, beyond any wish that it were otherwise, that the only way the light could pierce through the storm would be if she went outside, climbed to the upper balcony, and scraped the ice off.

Her legs felt as if they would collapse under her. The lump in her throat was so big she could hardly swallow. Somehow Jessie made it down the ladder. At the base of the light she grabbed the scrapers and hung them, again, around her neck.

"Don't think, Jessie," she told herself, pulling open the heavy metal door that led out onto the lower balcony. Wind and snow blew in the open doorway as she stepped out into the blizzard.

She struggled to close the door so the wind wouldn't blow out the light. The balcony was covered with ice and snow. Jessie's foot slid, and she grabbed hold of the railing. Her teeth chattered—with cold or fear, she didn't know which.

She looked up at the upper balcony with its skinny, low railing and shut her eyes. The wind came in blasts. Jessie could feel the lighthouse moving, giving slightly as the wind pushed against it. She gripped the iron railing with both hands. Why hadn't she thought to bring Granddad's heavy gloves? Well, it was too late now. If she went back down to the house, she'd never be able to force herself to come back up.

Jessie looked down. She couldn't help herself. It was as if something were pulling her down to the rocks, the rocks with the dark waves crashing over them, the rocks at the foot of the lighthouse. She had never heard the wind and the waves roaring so loudly, howling like gigantic beasts. The clang of the fog bell sounded distant, covered up by the sounds of the storm. From out on the lake, through sheets of ice and snow, came a long whistle. Jessie could see the shadowy form of a steamer being tossed up and down on the waves.

Could the captain see the light? Jessie looked up. The ice made the light look yellow and far away. She clutched the cords of the ice scrapers. Then she remembered the ladder. She would have to drag the wooden ladder out onto this balcony and hook it over the railing above her before she could even get up to the windows.

Out on the lake, the steamer's whistle blew again. Jessie pushed open the door to get back into the lighthouse. And there was Omie.

24

The sight of the old woman blocking the doorway was so unexpected, so out of place up at the top of the light, that it made Jessie stumble back onto the icy balcony.

"Fallen down, fallen down." Omie wobbled her head sadly back and forth.

Suddenly Jessie was somewhere else. She was a little girl with cold hands playing with her dog on the ice-crusted snow blanketing the beach. It was a gray day with snow in the air. Uncle Jim was on the upper balcony of the lighthouse. His arm moved up and down as he scraped the ice off the tall windows.

Her dog barked, and she turned to see Omie struggling down the beach toward her. Every step Omie took left a deep footprint in the snow. Her breath sent out clouds of steam that hung in the air.

"Jessie, meine Jessie," she said, opening her arms. *"Home, kommen home."*

"I'm not *your* Jessie. No, I'm not!" she cried, backing away.

Her little dog circled them, barking, barking.

Then Omie caught hold of her and hugged her close. She felt as if she were suffocating inside Omie's damp, smelly shawl.

"Leave me alone!" she cried, trying to fight her way out of the woman's embrace.

"Uncle Jim!" she shouted. "Uncle Jim!"

At the top of the lighthouse, he turned and looked down. "Omie!" he yelled.

He stepped over the rail and started climbing down the ladder. But then something happened, something awful happened, and he was falling . . . somersaulting down . . . down. Omie's strong arms let go of her. And everything was quiet. Quiet except for the sound of the gray waves slapping against the icy rocks. All this Jessie saw in an instant.

Then she was back, standing on the windswept lower balcony with Omie in the doorway. Jessie screamed, her cry piercing the curtain of the blizzard and bouncing off the rocks below. Omie backed into the round room at the top of the lighthouse.

"Omie! You killed him! You killed my Uncle Jim, didn't you? You made him fall!" Jessie felt the words strangling her. "Why did you grab me? You made me yell for him. That made him fall. Didn't it, Omie? Didn't it?"

The old woman rocked sadly back and forth, her head bowed.

"I hate you, Omie! I hate you!" Jessie shouted, her voice choked. "I never want to see you again!"

Omie lowered her head, not meeting Jessie's eyes. She backed down the stairs, her large body filling the opening. When her gnarled fingers let go of the rim, Jessie banged the hatch shut.

She lifted the wooden ladder from its alcove beside the door, and her mother's gloves fell from one of the rungs. She shoved her trembling hands into the soft leather and then pushed the ladder through the door and out onto the slippery balcony. Again she struggled to pull the door shut, and it finally clanged against its metal frame.

Inside her grandfather's clothes, she was drenched with sweat. Looking up, Jessie lifted the wooden ladder until its metal hooks grabbed the top of the iron railing. She shook the ladder. It seemed to be latched securely. Pressing herself against the rungs of the ladder, she inched her way upward.

"Don't look down. Just don't look down," she told herself. Rung after rung, she climbed. Now she was at eye level with the balcony. With her gloved hand she brushed off the snow. The knobby iron balcony under it was, as she feared, covered with a layer of ice. Hugging the ladder, she scraped at the ice in front of her.

Now was the hardest part, going up the final rungs and stepping over the top of the ladder and down onto the balcony. "Just don't think, Jessie, just don't think," she told herself.

As she raised her left leg over the railing, a gust of icy wind whipped around the lighthouse, almost knocking her off-balance. Sleet pelted her face. Jessie gripped the railing. Squinting her eyes, she stepped over the top of the ladder and down onto the balcony.

For what seemed like a long while, she huddled between the ice-covered windows and the ladder, unable to move. It was the burst of anger toward Omie that had gotten her up here, but now that was gone, torn out of her by the wind and the exertion of the climb. Now her anger was replaced by overwhelming, sickening fear.

Even though Jessie knew that the worst thing she could do would be to look down, she couldn't help herself. It was so far down to the ground, so far for Uncle Jim to have fallen. She was sure she knew how Uncle Jim had died.

"Uncle Jim, help me," she prayed. "Don't let me fall." She thought of her uncle and her grandfather up here on the balcony on icy, stormy nights like this one. "Help me, help me," she prayed.

Taking one of the scrapers that hung from her neck, Jessie began to scrape the ice off the windows. If they had been clear, the light would have been so blinding she would have had to shield her eyes or look away, but now it seemed as if the light were covered with a thick, white lampshade. There was a lull in the blizzard. Jessie hoped it would last. Kneeling on the balcony, she held on to the railing with one hand and scraped with the other. Slowly the light began to pierce through the glass.

"I'm doing it," Jessie said to herself. "I'm doing it." Her heart had begun to beat more slowly, steadily, no longer like the wings of a frightened, trapped bird. Jessie inched her way around the balcony. Finally, the bottom half of the glass was clear.

"Now you have to stand," Jessie said, coaching herself. "Just keep hold of the railing, and you'll be okay, Jessie. You'll be okay."

It was one thing to crawl around holding the railing, and another thing entirely to stand. When she stood, the railing only came up to Jessie's knees. The balcony seemed twice as slippery as it had when Jessie was kneeling on it. I'll have to scrape the ice off. I can't stand on ice, not up here, Jessie thought. So again, on her hands and knees, Jessie worked her way around the balcony. Finally it was as clear of ice as she could get it.

Her right hand ached so badly, it was almost useless. But it could hold on to the railing. "Hold on for dear life," Jessie said, repeating one of her grandmother's favorite expressions. Had she known how Uncle Jim had died? Jessie was sure her grandmother knew he had fallen. But no one knows why he fell, thought Jessie, no one but Omie and I. Jessie scraped up and down, up and down, shaving the ice off the upper part of the windows with her left hand, holding on to the railing for dear life with her right.

Up and down, up and down, *fallen down, fallen down* . . . Jessie was horrified to find herself repeating Omie's chant.

25

The panes of glass were finally clear. Once again, the light pierced the darkness. The wind still ripped at the lighthouse, but the blizzard seemed to have ended.

Jessie's arms felt as though they had weights attached to them. All she wanted to do was lie down on the balcony and rest.

"You'll freeze to death up here," Jessie told herself. "You have to get inside." But that meant climbing over the railing and going down the ladder, the same ladder that had slipped, sending Uncle Jim . . .

Jessie forced herself to stop thinking and just do what she had to. Her arms and hands were so stiff from the scraping, from the cold, she could hardly make them move. When she grabbed the top of the railing, the light dazzled her with its brightness. She stepped backward. Her right foot found the top rung of the ladder, but when she swung her left foot over the railing, everything started to slide.

The light disappeared. Reaching out, Jessie grabbed—at nothing. Then her right hand connected with a railing, slid down it, and stopped with a jerk that almost made her let go. She was dangling in the air, her legs thrashing back and forth, her feet trying to find something solid to stand on.

Where was the lower balcony that should have broken her fall? Then Jessie realized with absolute horror that she was hanging from the railing of the lower balcony, hanging by one hand over nothing, nothing but empty, dark space.

She couldn't scream; she couldn't do anything. Everything had stopped, frozen. When a sharp pain shot through Jessie's right arm, she found her voice. She screamed and then screamed again.

"Oh, God!" she prayed. She could think, pray, nothing beyond those words. Her arm ached. She felt her body grow heavier and heavier, pulling on her right arm, pulling on the one hand that held her dangling above the blackness. The stiff fingers inside her gloved hand, the fingers that seemed to belong to someone else, were opening.

"No!" Jessie screamed. She lunged up into the blackness with her left hand. Fumbling stiffly, frantically, her hand found the bottom of the rail—just in time.

Before, everything seemed to be happening as if in a terrible dream. But now Jessie was completely alert, aware. She willed her right arm to rise. She made her fingers open and grab the railing again. Now that she was holding on with both hands, she looked up at the underside of the lower balcony.

Slowly she moved her feet up and down along the slippery sides of the lighthouse. Somewhere, somewhere there was an iron pipe that curved around the outside of the light, a pipe that could give her a toehold, that could let her take her weight from her arms and hands, which were getting so stiff and numb they were almost beyond her control.

When it seemed as if she could hold on no longer, her right foot found the pipe, then her left foot. Jessie pressed both feet hard against the curving walls of the lighthouse. The pipe was small and slippery, but she could stand on it and, for a moment, almost rest.

"Hold on, Jessie. Hold on. Think!" she told herself over and over again. If she could somehow work her way up the rails and grab the top part of the railing, she could hoist herself over it and fall onto the safety of the balcony.

Her numb, frozen hands would have to work. They would have to work as they'd never worked before. She clenched them as hard as she could around the rail and then unclenched them just a bit, over and over again. Soon some warmth and, with it, some feeling began to return. Trying to concentrate all her strength into her arms, Jessie began to move her hands up the rails. But the round vertical rails were as slippery as icicles, and, as soon as her hands bore the full weight of her body, she slid back down. With growing desperation, Jessie realized that by herself she could not get back up on the balcony. But who could help her? Her mother was on the divan in the sitting room, asleep or unconscious with pain. The wind blasted Jessie's freezing body.

"Help!" she screamed. "Help!"

She tried once more to inch her hands up the rails, but again they slid down. She lost her footing on the pipe and once more swung out over nothingness, her legs dangling in a distorted dance. Her grandfather's cap blew off her head. Finally Jessie's feet found the pipe. With her whole body trembling, she resumed her precarious position. She looked down. The cap was just a small dark spot on the snow-covered rocks far below.

"Help! Help!" she screamed again. She knew she couldn't hang on much longer. Her arm muscles were starting to cramp. Her legs felt as though they were going to buckle under her at any moment.

Over the wind and the crashing waves, Jessie heard a sound above her, the sound of the iron door opening.

26

"Help! Help me!" Jessie shouted. "I'm over the railing! Help!" Jessie craned her neck backward to look up. All she could see was the underside of the balcony.

"Mama!" she yelled. "I'm over here! I can't hang on!"

Jessie closed her eyes and strained to keep her hold just one more minute, just one more second. Opening her eyes, it was Omie's face she saw, Omie peering over the railing at her.

"Help me, Omie!" Jessie cried. "Please . . . help me!"

Omie swayed back and forth, clutching the top rail. With a sudden movement, she bent over the railing and grabbed Jessie's right wrist. Then leaning way over, she grabbed Jessie's left wrist. Jessie's fingers let go of the railing. She shut her eyes. She felt her heart stop.

For a horrible instant, Omie seemed to lose her balance, and it seemed to Jessie that both she and Omie were going to fall head over heels down to the rocks below. But then Jessie felt herself being lifted up, up and over the railing. Omie fell backward against the curving wall of the lighthouse, tumbling Jessie onto the balcony's snowy floor.

Jessie lay on the icy metal, gasping for breath. Her heart hammered in her ears. She pressed her head back against the cold balcony. It felt so solid, so good. Jessie was crying . . . laughing. She wasn't going to fall. She wasn't going to die.

Jessie raised her head. Omie was still sitting where she had landed. She was chewing on her hand, her eyes wide. Jessie crawled over to her. Slowly, she helped her up.

Jessie was crying now. "Omie," she said, "I'm sorry. I'm sorry for what I said."

Omie rocked backed and forth. She opened her mouth as if she were going to speak but then closed it again.

Jessie took Omie's hand and led her back through the door of the lighthouse. She pushed the iron door shut and leaned against it. Oh, how wonderful that felt. Turning back to Omie, she saw, in the glow from the light, tears trickling down the wrinkles of the old woman's face.

Taking both of Omie's gnarled, bare hands in her gloved ones, Jessie said, "Omie, we didn't fall. Because of you, we didn't fall. You saved my life, Omie."

Omie looked hard at Jessie as if she were trying to remember. Her own little girl named Jessie? Uncle Jim falling? Or was she thinking about what had just happened? She looked puzzled and sad, a mixture of both.

"You were so good, Omie," Jessie said and then corrected herself. "You *are* good, Omie." She squeezed the old woman's hands.

A smile spread across Omie's face. "Good," she repeated. "Good, Omie. Good, Jessie."

And Jessie found herself, for the second time in her life, clutched in Omie's strong arms.

27

The wind continued to blow, but the storm had spent itself. For a while, Jessie and Omie just sat on the wonderful, solid, iron floor of the room under the light. Jessie pressed her back, her head, against the wall that curved around her like a protecting arm. Slowly, warmth was returning to her fingers and toes. The fall, the horror of dangling over empty black space, Omie grabbing her and pulling her up—seemed unreal. It all seemed to have happened to someone else.

Although Jessie was beyond exhaustion, she knew there was work to be done. She stood and flexed her stiff arms and her sore fingers. On legs that were still a bit wobbly, she climbed up to the lantern. Shielding her eyes from the blinding light, she carefully unfastened the lantern's door. She could see that the oil in the lamp would only last another hour. She would have to get a new lamp ready.

"Omie," she said, "we need to go down now."

The old woman nodded and, with Jessie's help, rose to her feet. Jessie opened the hatch, and Omie slowly began backing down the winding steps.

The watch room was freezing cold. Jessie's kerosene lantern was still burning, or was it the one Omie had carried up? Jessie held it up to check the oil inside the brass long-necked pouring can. The lard oil she needed for the lantern's new lamp had hardened into a white lump. She would have to heat it.

With Omie carrying the lantern and Jessie the pouring can, they made their way down the steps. Omie moved slowly, so it took a while for them to make the descent. With Jessie matching her pace to Omie's, they walked through the passageway and into the kitchen.

Jessie didn't know who was more surprised, she or Mr. Hostetler, who turned abruptly from the cookstove where he was pouring boiling water into the teapot. He set the kettle down hard and stared at the two of them.

Jessie looked down at her grandfather's uniform, the gold buttons shining in the lamplight. "Mr.—Mr. Hostetler, I can explain," she stammered.

Still staring at Jessie, he took the lantern from Omie's hands, extinguished the flame, and set it on the shelf above the stove.

"Well," he began, "well . . ." but Jessie was following Omie into the sitting room.

"My mother," she whispered over her shoulder. But in the lamplight she could see her mother was sleeping peacefully. Omie settled herself in Granddad's chair and began rocking quietly back and forth. From the kitchen doorway, Mr. Hostetler motioned for Jessie to join him.

"Here, sit down," he said, pulling a chair out from the table for her as if it were afternoon and he was in his own house. "Your mother's going to be fine." He took the long-necked oilcan out of Jessie's hands. "Now, what do I do with this?"

"Oh," Jessie said, suddenly having difficulty keeping her mind focused. "Please put it in a pan of hot water. It's so cold that the oil hardened. I need it for the light. But, Mr. Hostetler, why are you here?"

"First things first," he declared. Taking a large pan from its hook on the wall, he poured the rest of the kettle's boiling water into it and then set the oilcan in its center. A cloud of steam rose up around it. "That should do," he said. "Now for some tea." He poured two cups and settled himself in a chair across from Jessie. He watched as she put both her hands around the cup, closed her eyes, and breathed in the warm steam. Then, putting his hands on his legs, he leaned forward. "To answer your question, Jessie . . ."

At the sound of the serious tone of his voice, Jessie sat up, her eyes wide open. She could have gone to sleep breathing in the smell of the tea, the cup warming her hands.

"To answer your question," he began again, "during the blizzard—it must have been after midnight—I couldn't sleep for thinking about you and your mother here by yourselves. I was worried about what fool things you might be trying to do." He paused and shook his head. "From the looks of your mother's ankle and that uniform you're wearing, I can just imagine what your jobs were tonight."

Jessie felt like crying, blubbering like a baby, but she swallowed the lump in her throat and blinked back her tears. Straightening herself, she said in a small voice that shook just a little, "I had to do it. There was no one else. I had to get the ice off. It was blocking the light."

Mr. Hostetler's eyes widened, and Jessie was afraid he was going to start into a tirade again about the irresponsible Lighthouse Service not sending them help. Instead, he looked at her, in the almost stern way her grandfather often did, and then said, "I guess I owe you an apology for what I said yesterday afternoon. About you just being a help in the kitchen. Although, mind you, I'm not saying I approve. You know, if your grandfather were here . . ."

In her mind, Jessie saw her grandfather, her grandmother, Uncle Jim. Now the tears spilled out of her eyes. "Mr. Hostetler, I know how Uncle Jim died. When I was out on the balcony, and all of a sudden Omie was there in the doorway, I remembered everything. I screamed, and Uncle Jim—"

Mr. Hostetler motioned her to stop. "I know how your

Uncle Jim died, Jessie. I was on the beach that day. I saw Omie grab you and hug you. I heard you yell. I saw your Uncle Jim fall."

"You knew?" Jessie asked in disbelief. "You knew all this time? Did everyone know? My mother? Helen? Papa? Grandma and Granddad?"

"Yes, Jessie, everyone knew what happened."

"Did they know that Omie thought I was her little girl and that she was trying to take me away with her?" Jessie asked, her lower lip trembling.

"Oh," Mr. Hostetler said, taking Jessie's small hands in his large ones. "No. No one knew that."

"But," Jessie stopped, searching for the right words, "didn't they blame me for yelling, for making Uncle Jim—" She couldn't say the word.

"Jessie, Jessie," Mr. Hostetler said, "no one ever blamed you. You were only five years old. Omie frightened you. And now I know how badly she frightened you."

"But when I was older, why didn't anyone tell me when I asked them what had happened to Uncle Jim?"

"I'm sure they didn't see any good coming of it—of your knowing, of your remembering." Mr. Hostetler shook his head and sighed. Letting go of Jessie's hands, he ladled sugar from the table's sugar bowl into his tea and stirred it. He was quiet for a moment, staring into his cup. "It was terribly, terribly icy that day. My wife fell, and I thought she'd broken her leg. I came down to the lighthouse to get your grandfather. You know, he could have been a doctor, he was so good at fixing people up."

Jessie was hearing and yet at the same time not hearing, not understanding. "Jessie," Mr. Hostetler said, taking her hands again, "no one blamed you. And, for pity's sake, don't go blaming yourself, not now after all these years. It wasn't your fault. Don't you ever think it was."

Not her fault. Maybe Uncle Jim's death wasn't her fault, but now Jessie's mind replayed this horrible night and her fear, how she had almost abandoned the light. How many lives might have been lost because of something that *was* her fault?

"Mr. Hostetler," Jessie began, "there's something I have to tell you—something that *was* my fault, that *is* my fault." She stopped and swallowed hard. "The Lighthouse Service hasn't sent help because they don't know we need help. They don't even know Granddad is dead."

"What?" Mr. Hostetler looked at her in disbelief. "Surely your mother sent word."

Jessie hurried to finish before she lost her courage. "I didn't mail her letter, at least not the way I was supposed to by putting it on the mailboat." Tea spilled over the rim of the cup as she set it back down in its saucer. "I—I mailed it by putting it in a canning jar and throwing it into the lake." Jessie couldn't bring herself to meet her old neighbor's eyes.

The silence between them was broken only by the ticking of the clock in the sitting room and Omie's rocking. Finally Jessie looked up. Mr. Hostetler nodded. Stroking the gray stubble on his chin, he said, "You've grown up a bit tonight, haven't you, Jessie?"

Jessie nodded, unable to speak.

Mr. Hostetler walked over to the kitchen window and, moving the curtains aside, looked out into the darkness. "If I were a lad of twelve, Jessie, I might have done the same thing with the letter, not wanting to lose the light. But I don't know if I were a lad of twelve whether I would have, *could* have, done what you did tonight to keep that light burning."

"I didn't want to do it. I almost . . ." Jessie stood up, almost knocking over her chair.

"But you did it," Mr. Hostetler interrupted. "It shows what

kind of cloth you're made of." He came over to her and straightened the jacket on her shoulders. "Those clothes might just fit you one of these days."

Jessie had forgotten she was wearing her grandfather's uniform. She shuddered when she remembered what had happened to his cap.

"You were right, Mr. Hostetler, yesterday at your house, when you said that Mama and I can't do it alone. I know that now."

"Jessie?" It was her mother's voice calling her.

28

The sitting room was warm. In the lamplight, Jessie could see that some color had returned to her mother's face. Beside the fireplace, Omie sat in the rocking chair, sound asleep.

Jessie knelt to hug her mother.

"Jessie?" she said, raising her head from the pillow. "Why are you wearing Granddad's uniform?"

"Everything is fine, Mama," Jessie said and seated herself on a stool beside her mother. "Please don't worry." She could see that her mother's ankle was still swollen. Just the sight of it made Jessie wince.

"I don't think that ankle is broken, Mrs. Lafferty," said Mr. Hostetler, placing a cup of tea on the table beside her. "Just a bad sprain would be my guess."

Carefully pushing herself up to a sitting position, she said, "How can I thank you for coming over here in the middle of the night to help us?"

"Well, I don't know that I've done anything other than make up the fire in here and boil some water. But you can be mighty proud of this daughter of yours. When you're feeling a little better," he continued, "Jessie might tell you why she had to put on that uniform."

"Jessie?" her mother looked up at her quickly, questioning.

"I will tell you about it, Mama, just not now." Jessie closed her eyes for a second and then looked over at Mr. Hostetler. "Oh!" she said. "The oil. I almost forgot I have to put a new lamp in the light, Mama. You just rest."

At the mention of the light, her mother sat up straight, completely alert. "The storm, Jessie, the ice—"

"The storm's over, Mama. The light is fine. You don't need to worry." There would be time—time to talk about everything. She straightened the afghans on her mother and gave her a kiss. Over by the fireplace, Omie coughed, bolted upright, and began rocking. The chair creaked, and she smiled. Jessie crossed the room and stood beside her.

"Are you all right, Omie?" Jessie asked.

The old woman nodded and kept rocking.

Jessie's mother looked at the two of them. "Jessie?" she said. Then, shaking her head, she closed her eyes and lay back against the pillows.

"Put me to work," Mr. Hostetler said.

Jessie thought for a few seconds. "You could wind the fog bell, Mr. Hostetler. Even though it's pretty clear now, there are probably still some squalls, and the bell might help some ships out in the channel. Keeping the fog bell ringing was Omie's job tonight."

"Omie's job?" Mr. Hostetler asked.

"*One* of Omie's jobs," Jessie corrected herself, remembering Omie's hands pulling her to safety.

"I'll see you in the morning, when I've finished watching the light," Jessie said. She looked at all of them, there in the lamplight, in the warm sitting room. Our house doesn't seem so empty and cold anymore, she thought.

In the kitchen, the lard had melted in the oilcan. Jessie lit her lantern and, with both hands full, made her way through the passageway and up the curving steps of the lighthouse.

29

After she prepared the new lamp, Jessie slowly made her way up the ladder to the lantern. How will I ever tell Mama about tonight? she wondered. She remembered a story her grandmother had told about a woman whose brown hair turned white in an instant when she had a terrible scare. Jessie looked at her untidy braids, not white, not yet. Maybe when I have time to sit and think about what happened, Jessie thought. Maybe I'd better not tell Mama everything, at least not till she's better and, for sure, not till we have some help or . . . Jessie didn't want to think of that other possibility, at least not right now.

Carefully, she placed the new lamp inside the lantern and closed the brass-hinged door. The circles of flame danced through the prisms of the lantern in a kaleidoscope of light.

Jessie turned to look out the windows—now clear because she had gone out onto the icy balcony and scraped them, scraped them so the light could shine out across the treacherous Manitou Channel—all the way to the dark, low hills of the mainland. She touched the curved prisms of the lantern. With the cuff of her Granddad's uniform she rubbed the brass fittings—polished, taken care of for so many years by her family.

What does it mean to be brave? Jessie had always thought of her father sailing his ship through the wild waves. She thought of her mother, her grandfather, her Uncle Jim, and the courage it took to climb that ladder to the icy balcony around the light. But there was another kind of courage, one she hadn't comprehended as little as one day ago, the kind of courage it takes to write a letter and send it, realizing that you might be sending away forever everything you know and love.

Mr. Hostetler was right, Jessie thought. She *had* done some growing up overnight. In two days, the mailboat would come on its twice-a-month trip to the island. Jessie knew, no matter what it might mean for her and her family, that she would send her mother's second letter to the Lighthouse Service.

In the half-moon-shaped harbor, she could see the silhouettes of ships, schooners, and steamers—how many, she didn't know—rocking in the protected waters. Looking to the east, she saw the faintest crimson streak in the sky over Pyramid Point. In less than an hour it will be light, she thought.

As she turned to leave the lantern room, Jessie spotted a schooner, its sails puffed with the wind, cutting its way toward the safety of the harbor. Through habit, Jessie counted the masts—three. Then she stopped and leaned closer to the window, squinting, trying to bring the ship closer. There was something very familiar about this three-masted schooner. Could it be her father's ship, the *Isabella*? She was almost sure that it was.
Jessie hurried down the ladder and through the hatch, clanging the iron door above her, closing it to protect the light.

The End

Acknowledgments

Of great assistance when I needed information about South Manitou Island's lighthouses were Kimberly Mann, historical architect, and Bill Herd, National Park ranger, at the Sleeping Bear Dunes National Lakeshore office in Empire, Michigan.

For help with various drafts of the story, I must thank my fellow writers and friends Jane Freeman, Robyn Eversole, and Marc Harshman, and my husband, Kim. Any mistakes or omissions are my own.

For their encouragement and friendship I would like to thank Linda Kucan, Sandy Vrana, Phyllis Wilson Moore, Debbie Benedetti, Mary Loomis, Rosi Miller, Charley Hively, and countless other teachers, librarians, and friends who have been so supportive.

With special thanks to my family—the West Virginia Egans and the Michigan Smuckers.

Author's Note

The characters in this story are fictional, and the life of South Manitou Island has been changed in several instances for the sake of the story, but the lighthouse is real. Several years ago, my family and I camped on this lovely island in Lake Michigan. On a sunny day in August we followed a National Park ranger up the winding steps of the South Manitou Island Lighthouse and out onto the lower balcony that circles the top of the lighthouse. The view from up so high was at the same time breathtakingly beautiful and very scary.

Stories often begin with a writer asking the question: "What if?" And so this story began with *What if it were November, a stormy, sleety night in November in the nineteenth century, with ice building up in layers on the windows of the lighthouse? What if I were only twelve years old and afraid to be at the top of the lighthouse even on a sunny summer day? What if something had happened to the lightkeeper and I was the only one who could climb the ladder to the upper balcony and scrape off the ice so the light could shine through to warn the ships?* I asked these and many other questions, until Jessie Lafferty, her mother, Omie, and the other characters in my story came to life.

The story begins in early October 1871. The year has been very dry. Newspaper accounts report fires burning in the forests around Lake Michigan all summer and into the fall. On the evening of October 8, 1871, two catastrophic fires ignite. One of these, the great Chicago fire, will destroy the city and claim up to three hundred lives. The other fire, less well known but far more deadly, will rage around Green Bay, Wisconsin, burning 1.25 million acres of forest and destroying the lumber town of Peshtigo. Possibly as many as two thousand people will die. Smoke from the fires spreads like a blanket all the way up Lake Michigan to the Straits of Mackinac.

In my story, the fires are the reason for the inspector's hurried visit warning the lightkeepers to be ready. There really was a lightkeeper who piled pots and pans on his lap to keep himself awake to ring the fog bell for the three days and nights the lake was covered with the smoke. This is recorded in Charles K. Hyde's *The Northern Lights: Lighthouses of the Upper Great Lakes*. The description of Patrick Malloy's rescue of the crew and passengers of the ship that ran aground on the shoals near the island is derived from this same book.

Instructions to Light-Keepers, a photoreproduction of the 1902 edition of *Instructions to Light-Keepers and Masters of Light-House Vessels,* was an invaluable resource not only for reconstructing the operation of the complicated equipment of the lighthouse but also for becoming acquainted with the myriad rules and regulations that governed both the care of the light and the daily work, and, therefore, life of the lightkeeper.

The Need for Lighthouses on the Great Lakes

The Great Lakes were the highways of the 1800s. Water travel throughout all the Great Lakes was made possible by the St. Mary's Falls Ship Canal. Better known as the Soo Locks, it opened at Sault Ste. Marie in 1855. Raw materials such as lumber, coal, iron, and copper as well as farm products moved east on this vast lake waterway. Manufactured goods and thousands of immigrants moved west. The population in what is now the states of Ohio, Michigan, Indiana, Illinois, and Wisconsin increased from around 800,000 in 1820 to more than nine million by 1860.

As shipping and passenger travel increased, so did the frequency of shipwrecks. Every year, more lives and cargo were lost. Those unfamiliar with the Great Lakes often fail to realize how deadly storms can be on these inland seas. Sailors say the only difference between storms on the ocean and storms on the Lakes is the taste of the spray. During the winter of 1870–71, 214 people drowned on the Great Lakes. Between 1878 and 1898, almost six thousand ships were wrecked. There was an obvious need for lighthouses to guide ships to safe harbors and to warn them of dangerous rocks and shoals, the sandbars just below the water's surface.

The Manitou Passage

The Manitou Passage is the channel between South and North Manitou Islands and the mainland. Rather than sailing out into Lake Michigan to the west of the islands, ships traveled this passage as a shortcut between Chicago and the Straits of Mackinac. Using the passage also put them near the safety of South Manitou's harbor in case of stormy or foggy weather. On the map, the channel looks wide. The distance between South Manitou Island and the coastal fishing town of Leland is sixteen miles, but shoals, with their hidden sandbars, are scattered across it. The part of the channel that is deep enough for ships is very narrow. For sailing vessels, storms and heavy fog made finding and staying in the navigable part of the channel very difficult.

Before the end of the Civil War, more than twelve hundred ships sailed the passage. Often these ships made up to thirty-five trips each year. With all of this traffic on such dangerous water, some estimates put the number of ships lost in the Manitou Passage at more than two hundred.

The Lighthouses of South Manitou Island

Several factors combined to make a lighthouse on South Manitou Island necessary. Located on the heavily traveled and treacherous Manitou Passage, the island had the only deep harbor between Chicago and the island, a distance of 220 miles. Some accounts say that up to one hundred vessels, steamers, schooners, and other boats anchored in the harbor during storms. Also, because of its wood supply, South Manitou Island was an important refueling stop for wood-burning steamers whose boilers needed from one hundred to three hundred cords of wood for each trip through the lakes.

In 1838, Congress authorized five thousand dollars for the building of a lighthouse on the island. Work was begun in 1839 and the lighthouse was completed at the end of spring in 1840. It was a brick or stone one-story house with a separate tower for the light.

In 1858, the first lighthouse was replaced by a two-and-a-half-story brick house with the light placed above it on a wooden tower. A separate small building housed the fog signal. Although this light was sixty-four feet above the water level, it still wasn't high enough. From out on the lake the light was difficult to distinguish from the lights of the ships in South Manitou's harbor.

Because of the problem identifying the light, the increased traffic in the Manitou Passage, and the importance of the island's harbor, a recommendation was made in 1869 for the construction of a hundred-foot-tall lighthouse tower in front of the lightkeeper's house. This tower would have a stronger light, a third-order Fresnel lens, with a range of eighteen miles. Funds were approved, and construction began in 1871.

To support the tower, two hundred timbers, each a foot square, were driven seventy feet into the sand. The walls at the base of the tower are more than five feet thick and taper to less than three feet at the top. They are hollow, allowing the tower to sway slightly when buffeted by strong winds. The tower was connected to the lightkeeper's house by an enclosed brick passageway. In 1875 a steam-powered fog signal was installed in the fog signal building, replacing the earlier fog bell.

The beautiful South Manitou Island Lighthouse was state of the art for its time and was one of the highest on the Great Lakes. It and its many dedicated lighthouse keepers served the needs of the ships well. In 1935, the North Manitou Shoal Light was erected and later the South Manitou Shoal Lighted Gong Buoy, making the lighthouse unnecessary. The lighthouse was closed on December 12, 1958. Today it is a historical museum that is part of the Sleeping Bear Dunes National Lakeshore. During the warm weather months, National Park Service rangers conduct tours, explaining the important role the lighthouse played when ships depended on it for safe travel.

South Manitou Island Lighthouse, 1884

JOURNAL of Light Station at South Manitou Mich
June 1928

MONTH 19	DAY	RECORD OF IMPORTANT EVENTS AT THE STATION, BAD WEATHER, ETC.
	15	N.W. light to Calm Clear. Rekindled No 1 and painted part of side walk 2nd. Wimen on leave ans and Keeper returned to station ans
	16	S.W. Moderate and Clear. Finished white washing Tower and scrapped most all old white work off tower
	17	N.E. Mod Cloudy Sunday.
	18	N.E. fresh Cloudy. Washing windows and put up screens etc.
	19	N.E. Moderate white washing around base of dwelling hall way and finer
	20	S.W. Mod to light Cloudy and fog sounding signal and polishing brass in tower. Cleaned Boiler No 2.
	21	S.W. Mod and fog sounding part of day.
	22	N.E. Mod partly Cloudy Washed windows and finished putting up screens etc
	23	S.W. to West moderate and fog. Sounding and general saturdays scrubbing etc.
	24	S.W. W. N.W. Moderate and fog and cloudy. Sunday
	25	N.W. fresh to W. fresh and Cloudy. Cleaning up in fog and bell house etc.
	26	N.W. Mod Shifting to S.W. Mod partly Cloudy. Polishing brass in signal. Painted steam pump and painted hall floors and scrubbing painting in Keepers Kitchen etc.
	27	S.W. Mod to fresh partly Cloudy painted Tower steps and painted in Keepers Kitchen.
	28	North Moderate to fresh rain + fog. Painting white in quarters and sounding
	29	North fresh rain + fog N E Clear sounding and painted and Cleaned in quarters etc
	30	S.W. Moderate partly Cloudy and Haze. White washed bell house inside and painted smoke stacks and and black on landings on tower and scrubbing etc.

Page from the journal of the South Manitou Island Lighthouse light-keeper, recording the weather and duties performed, 1928.

2-MASTED SCHOONER — foremast, mainmast

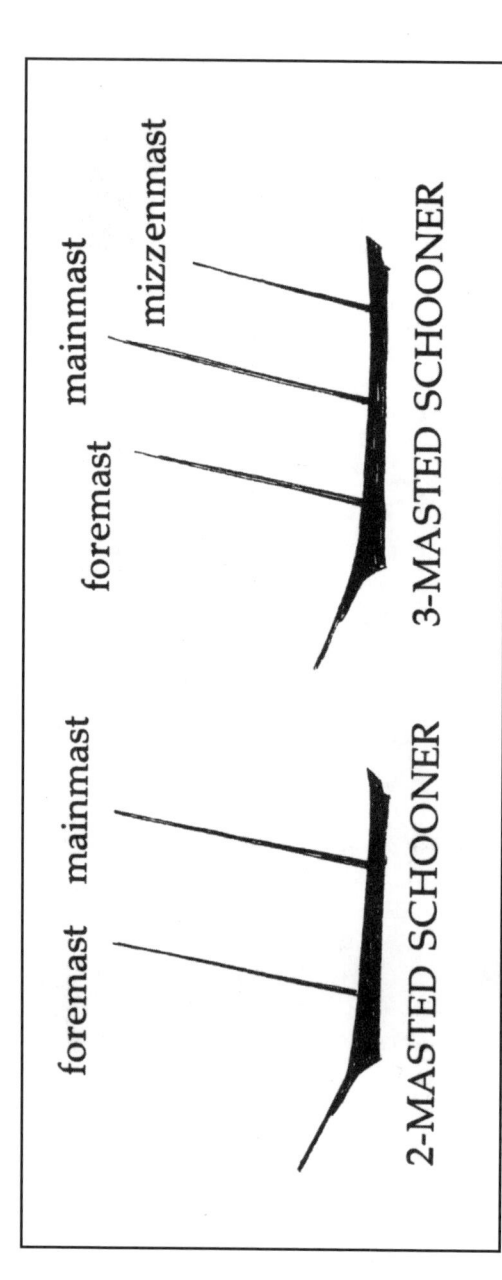

3-MASTED SCHOONER — foremast, mainmast, mizzenmast

Two types of schooners. A schooner has at least two masts—foremast and mainmast—with the mainmast being the taller. In the late 1800s, more than 2,000 schooners sailed the Great Lakes, carrying everything from lumber to potatoes. They could sail closer to the wind than square riggers and didn't need as large a crew.

NO.	NAME	LOSS DATE	CARGO	TYPE	NO.	NAME	LOSS DATE	CARGO	TYPE
1	Unknown			St.	22	H.D. Moore	9 Oct. 1907	Corn	Sch.
2	W. H. Gilcher	28 Oct. 1892	Coal	Sch.	23	Congress	5 Oct. 1904	Lum.	St.
3	Ostrich	28 Oct. 1892			24	Annie Vaught	21 Nov. 1892	Coal	Sch.
4	Unkown				25	Three Brothers	27 Sept. 1911	Lum.	St.
5	Gilbert Mollison	27 Oct. 1873	Corn	Sch.	26	L. Button		Lum.	Sch.
6	Equator	18 Nov. 1869	R.R. Ties	St.	27	J.Y. Scammon	8 Aug. 1854	Mix.	Brig.
7	Grand Turk		Corn		28	Ellen Spry	5 Nov. 1858		
8	J. L. Hurd		Posts	Sch.	29	C.L. Johnson			
9	Geneva	1859	Brick	Sch.	30	Queen of t' Lakes			
10	Troy		Glass		31	Montauk		Grain	Sch.
11	Pulaski	3 Oct. 1887		Sch.	32	L.M. 'Hubby		Mix.	Bark
12	Alva Bradley	3 Oct. 1854		Sch.	33	Francisco Morazon	1 Dec. 1960	Mix.	St.
13	Unknown				34	Walter L. Frost	4 Nov. 1903	Mix.	St.
14	H.G. Stamback			Brig	35	Unknown			
15	Josephine Dresden	27 Nov. 1909	Ballast	Sch.	36	Gold Hunter		Chi.	Sch.
16	Temperence			Sch.	37	General Taylor	Sept. 1862	Mix.	St.
17	Medota				38	J.S. Crouse	15 Nov. 1919	Lum.	St.
18	G. Knapp		Grain	Sch.	39	Flying Cloud		Coal	Sch.
19	R. P. Ralph		Lum.	St.	40	Westmoreland	7 Dec. 1854	Mix.	St.
20	Margaret Dall	16 Nov. 1906		Sch.	41	Florida	27 Aug. 1894		
21	Unknown				42	Rising Sun	29 Oct. 1918	Mac.	St.

Sch. = schooner   St. = Steamer   Chi. = China   Mix. = Mixed   Lum. = Lumber   Mac. = Machinery

List of shipwrecks in the Manitou Passage, Lake Michigan

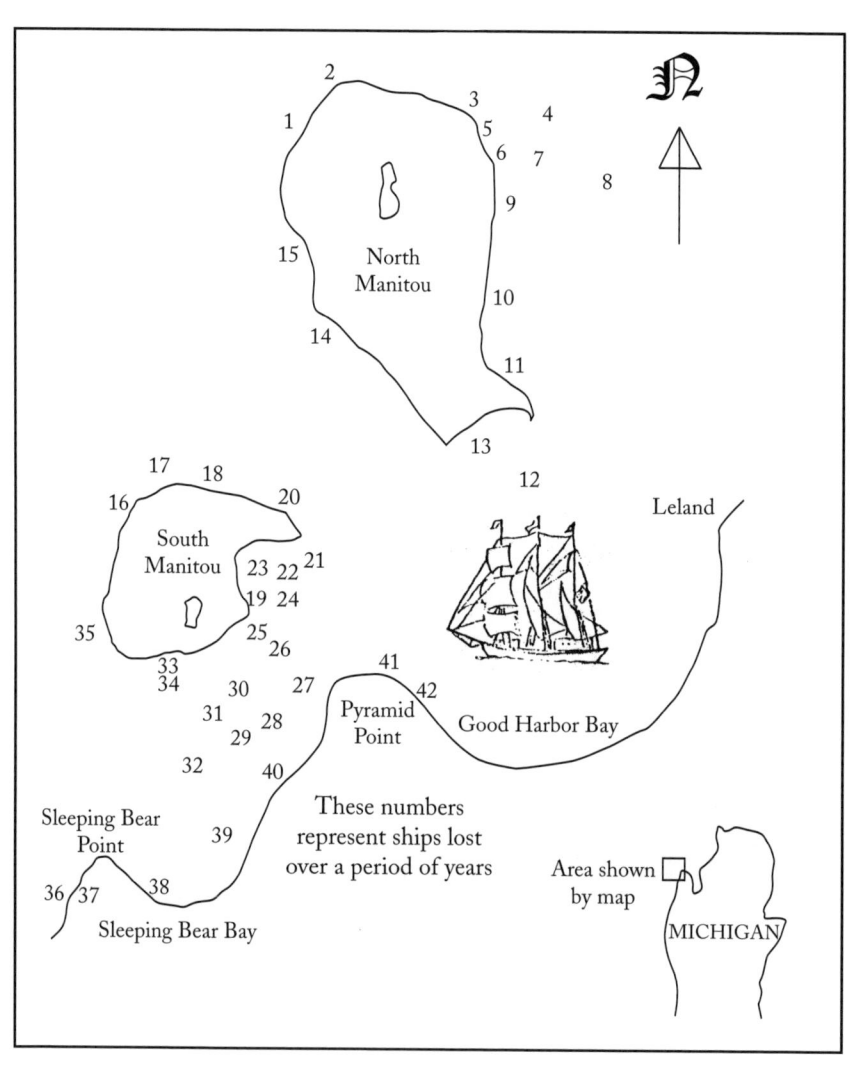

Map of shipwrecks in the Manitou Passage, Lake Michigan

SOUTH MANITOU ISLAND, GLEN ARBOR VICINITY, LEELANAU COUNTY, MICHIGAN

U.S. LIGHTHOUSE RESERVATION

SOUTH MANITOU HAS BEEN THE SITE OF BEACONS PROVIDING SAFE PASSAGE TO SHIPS SINCE 1839. THE ORIGINAL 1839 LIGHT STATION WAS BUILT TO MARK THE SOUTHERNMOST POINT OF THE MANITOU PASSAGE OF LAKE MICHIGAN, THE MOST IMPORTANT ROUTE TO THE STRAITS OF MACKINAC. TOGETHER WITH THE LIGHT ON NORTH MANITOU ISLAND, THE TWO BEACONS GUIDED SHIPS THROUGH THE NARROW PASSAGE BETWEEN THE ISLANDS AND THE LEELEANAU PENINSULA OF MICHIGAN. IN 1858, RECOGNIZING THE NEED FOR GREATER SAFETY, THE U S LIGHTHOUSE SERVICE ERECTED A NEW LIGHTHOUSE WITH A FOURTH ORDER FRESNEL LENS. THE TWO STORY BRICK RESIDENCE ALSO BUILT AT THAT TIME STILL STANDS.

SHIPPING CONTINUED TO INCREASE IN THE SUBSEQUENT YEARS UNTIL EVENTUALLY THE RANGE OF THE 1858 LIGHT WAS NO LONGER ADEQUATE. THUS, IN 1871 THE CURRENT, TALLER CYLINDRICAL, MASONRY TOWER SUPPORTING A MORE LUMINOUS THIRD-ORDER FRESNEL LENS WAS BUILT. THE DESIGN OF THE CURRENT TOWER IS TYPICAL OF THOSE BUILT IN SCATTERED LOCATIONS ALONG THE GREAT LAKES DURING THE 19TH CENTURY, THUS REFLECTING THE STANDARDIZATION OF DESIGNS GENERATED BY THE U.S. LIGHTHOUSE BOARD.

CIRCA 1930, THE NORTH MANITOU LIGHTHOUSE, WHICH HAD SUPPLEMENTED THE SOUTH LIGHT, WAS SWEPT OFF ITS FOUNDATIONS AND A NEW LIGHT WAS BUILT ON A CRIB FURTHER OUT ON THE DANGEROUS SHOAL. THE "CRIB LIGHT" MADE THE SOUTH MANITOU LIGHTHOUSE OBSOLETE BECAUSE OF ITS CLOSER PROXIMITY TO THE PASSAGE. IN 1958, THE U.S. COAST GUARD CLOSED THE LIGHT STATION WHICH NOW SERVES AS AN INTERPRETIVE SITE WITHIN THE SLEEPING BEAR DUNES NATIONAL LAKESHORE.

AREA MAP
FROM SLEEPING BEAR DUNES NATIONAL PARK BROCHURE, GPO 1990-262-109/20004

SOUTH MANITOU ISLAND
LIGHTHOUSE LOCATION: UTM 16 570140 4984000

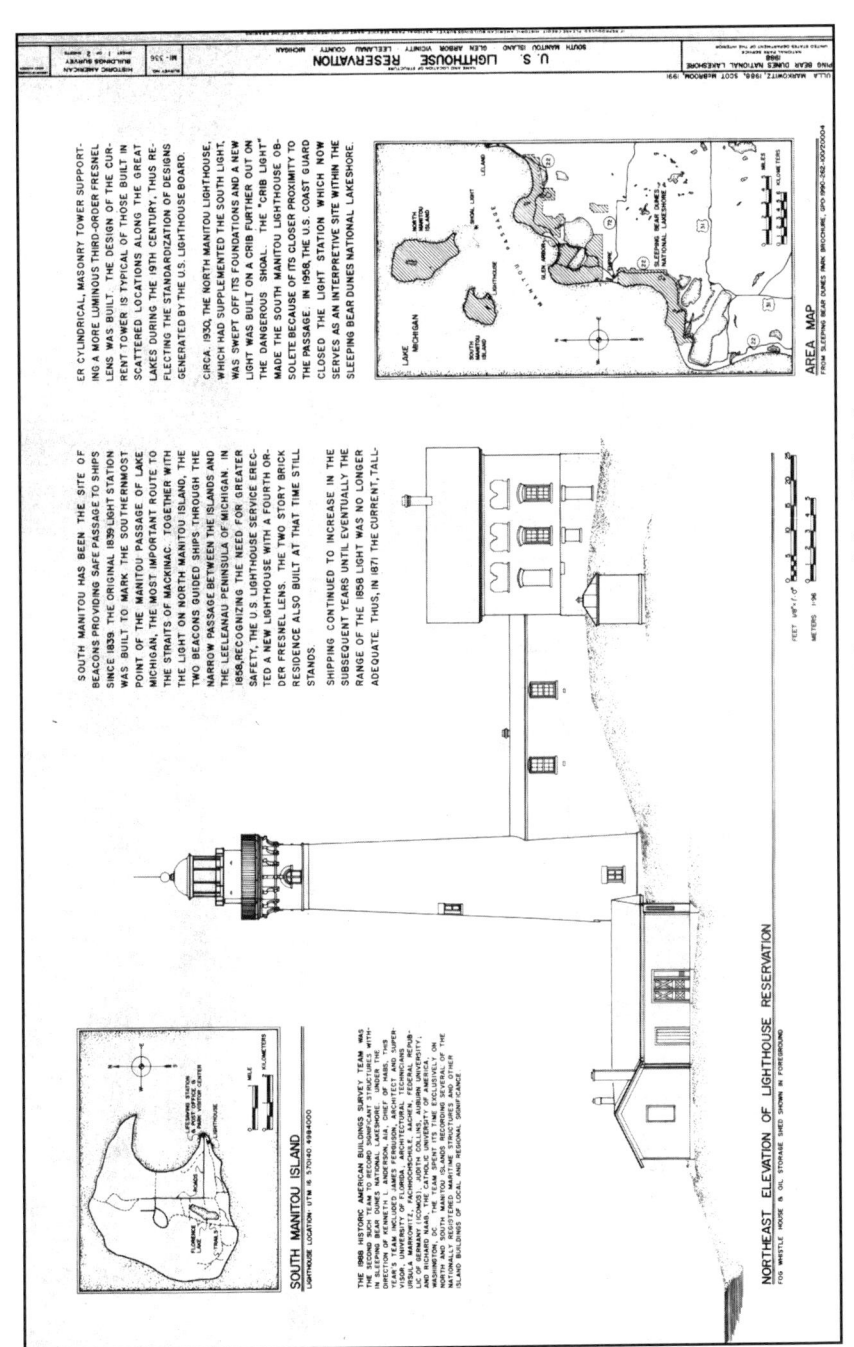

THE 1988 HISTORIC AMERICAN BUILDINGS SURVEY TEAM WAS THE SECOND SUCH TEAM TO RECORD SIGNIFICANT STRUCTURES WITHIN SLEEPING BEAR DUNES NATIONAL LAKESHORE. UNDER THE DIRECTION OF KENNETH L. ANDERSON, AIA, CHIEF OF HABS, THIS YEAR'S TEAM INCLUDED JAMES C. MASSEY, ARCHITECT AND SUPERVISOR; URSULA MARKOWITZ, RACHEL MANNING, AND SCOTT NEWBOURN, ARCHITECTURAL TECHNICIANS FROM THE CATHOLIC UNIVERSITY OF AMERICA, UNIVERSITY OF FLORIDA, AND RICHARD NASS, THE CATHOLIC UNIVERSITY OF AMERICA, UNIVERSITY OF GERMANY (ICOMOS); JUDITH COLLINS, AUBURN UNIVERSITY; WASHINGTON, DC. THE TEAM SPENT ITS TIME EXCLUSIVELY ON NORTH AND SOUTH MANITOU ISLANDS RECORDING SEVERAL OF THE NATIONALLY REGISTERED MARITIME STRUCTURES AND OTHER ISLAND BUILDINGS OF LOCAL AND REGIONAL SIGNIFICANCE.

NORTHEAST ELEVATION OF LIGHTHOUSE RESERVATION
FOG WHISTLE HOUSE & OIL STORAGE SHED SHOWN IN FOREGROUND

Northeast view of the South Manitou Island Lighthouse

The second South Manitou Island lighthouse built in 1858

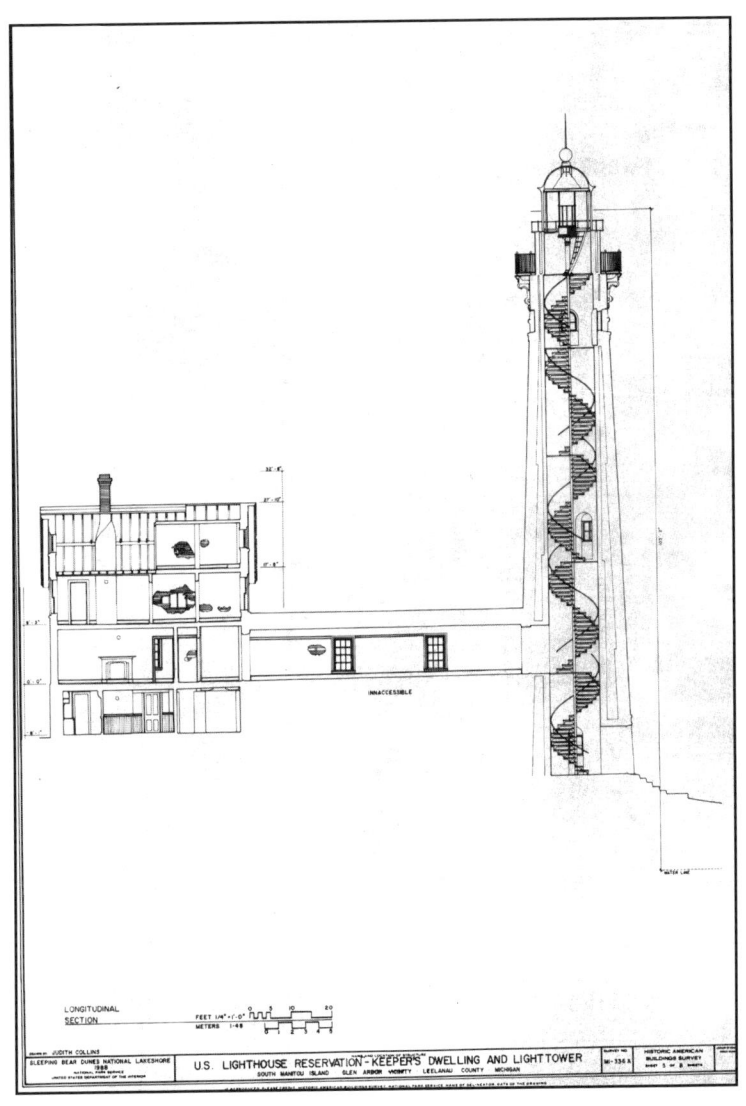

The third South Manitou Island lighthouse

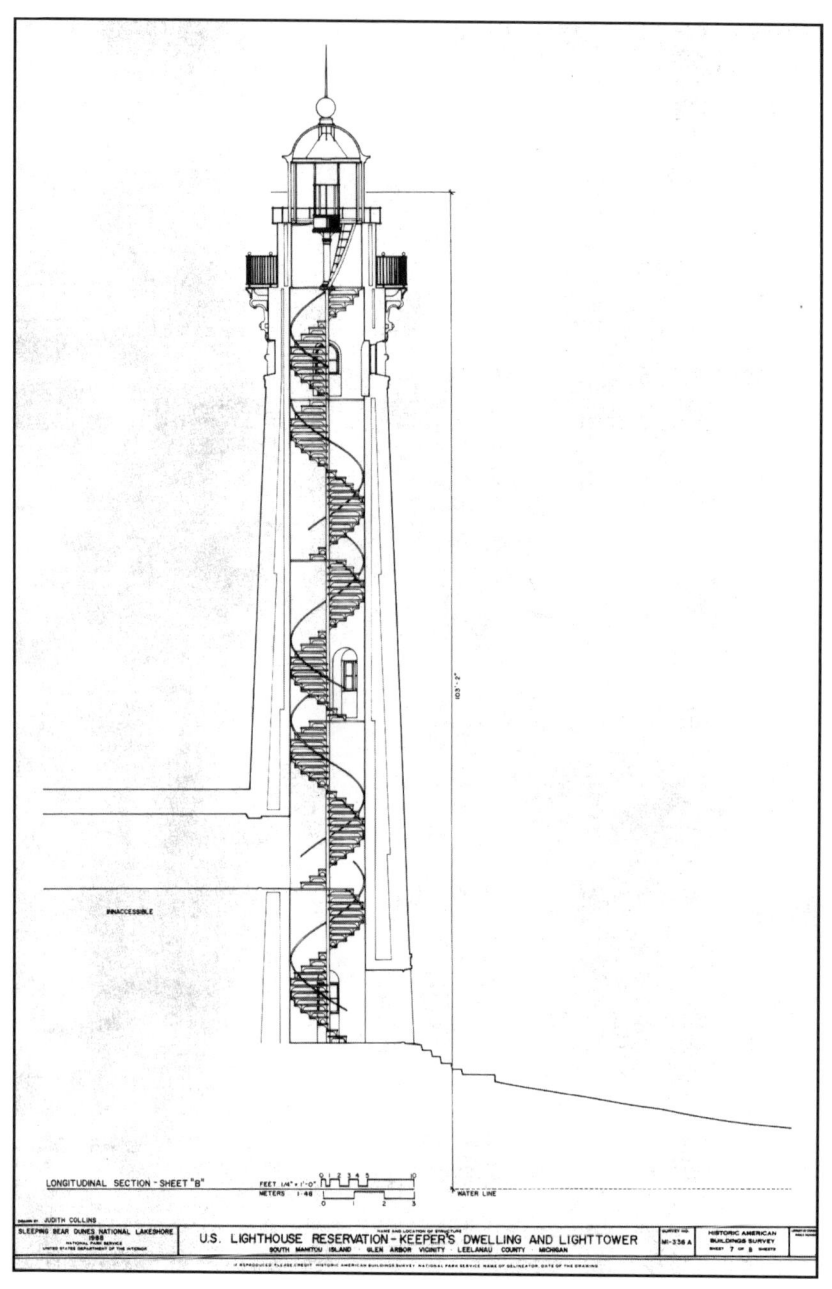

The South Manitou Island light tower

The South Manitou Island Lighthouse

View from the top of the South Manitou Island Lighthouse looking toward the harbor

View of the fog signal building as seen from the top of the South Manitou Island Lighthouse

View of the upper balcony surrounding the panes of glass around the lantern, as seen from the lower balcony of the South Manitou Island Lighthouse

View of the passageway and lightkeeper's house as seen from the top of the South Manitou Island Lighthouse

Looking up the spiral steps of the South Manitou Island Lighthouse

Sources for Information about South Manitou Island

Anderson, Charles M. *Isle of View: A History of South Manitou Island.* Frankfort, Mich.: J. B. Publications, 1979.

Great Lakes Lighthouse Keepers Association. *Instructions to Light-Keepers: A Photoreproduction of the 1902 Edition of "Instructions to Light-Keepers and Masters of Light-House Vessels."* Allen Park, Mich.: Great Lakes Lighthouse Keepers Association, 1989.

Hyde, Charles K. *The Northern Lights: Lighthouses of the Upper Great Lakes.* Lansing, Mich.: Two Peninsula Press, 1986.

Vent, Myron H. *South Manitou Island: From Pioneer Community to National Park.* 1973. Reprint, Conshohocken, Pa.: Eastern National Park and Monument Association, 1989.

Visitors' Guide to South Manitou Island. Mason, Mich.: Maritime Press, 1989.

About the Author

Photo by Sally Egan

Anna Egan Smucker makes her home in Bridgeport, West Virginia, but is a longtime summer resident of northern Michigan, where her husband's family has owned a cottage on Long Lake near Interlochen since the 1950s. Anna is the author of *Outside the Window* (Knopf, 1994) and *No Star Nights* (Knopf, 1989), which won the 1990 International Reading Association Children's Book Award in the Younger Reader category. In addition to writing, Anna gives author presentations and conducts writing workshops throughout the country.

Credits

South Manitou Lighthouse on pages vi–vii by Louise Bass, Traverse City, Mich.

Jessie's South Manitou Island on page viii by Anna Egan Smucker.

1884 lighthouse on page 112 from National Archives at College Park, College Park, Md., photograph no. 26-LG-53-37-2; "South Manitou Light Station," 1884.

Lightkeeper's journal on page 113 from "Journal of Light Station at South Manitou Michigan, June 1928 (days 15–30)"; Entry 80, Lighthouse Station Logs, 1897–1941; Records of the U.S. Coast Guard, Record Group 26; National Archives at National Archives Building, Washington, D.C.

Schooners on page 114 reprinted with permission from *Surfmen and Lifesavers* by Paul Giambarba (Centerville, Mass.: Scrimshaw, 1985), p. 112.

Map and chart on pages 115–116 reprinted with permission from *Isle of View: A History of South Manitou Island* by Charles M. Anderson (Frankfort, Mich.: J.B. Publications, 1979), pp. 28–29.

Architectural drawings on pages 117–120 courtesy Library of Congress, Prints and Photographs Division, Historic American Buildings Survey MICH, 45-GLAR, 8A.

Photos on pages 121–124 courtesy of Anna Egan Smucker.